C000252991

THINGS THAT MAKE THE HEART BEAT FASTER

To Vicky & John
Thank you for celebrating
my book launch with me

THINGS THAT
MAKE THE HEART
BEAT FASTER

Short Stories

João

João Morais

xxxx

11.10.2018

PARTHIAN

Parthian, Cardigan SA43 1ED
www.parthianbooks.com
First published in 2018
© João Morais 2018
All Rights Reserved
ISBN 978-1-912109-01-2
Editor: Susie Wild
Cover image from *Cardiff After Dark* by Maciej Dakowicz
Cover design by Syncopated Pandemonium
Typeset by Elaine Sharples
Printed in EU by Pulsio SARL
Published with the financial support of the Welsh Books Council
British Library Cataloguing in Publication Data
A cataloguing record for this book is available from the British Library.

Contents

The Pavement Poet   1

The Tea Party   12

The Anatomy of a Beating   20

Untitled (Text on Paper, 2018)   29

Asking a Shadow to Dance   40

Things That Make the Heart Beat Faster   49

One of the Cullens   63

The Nice Guy   74

The Visit   85

Yes Kung Fu   96

Notes   105

Acknowledgements   107

The Pavement Poet

It's the last day of the month and I still have money in the bank, and I can't help but feel that I've somehow failed at life. I make the most of it by getting a halloumi slammer and a raw coconut cacao bar for lunch, and I send Erin a picture to show her how I'm always eating vegan.

I'm sat on the big rock in the middle of the stone circle in the park, reading a review on my phone of the book Erin lent me. I'm reading a review so I can pretend to Erin that I could be arsed to read the whole thing, but I'm surrounded on all sides by screaming kids. They've been going back and forth like ants to the ice cream van on the edge of the grass, and now they're all so jumpy that they won't stop shouting at each other. The review goes on forever about the book's relevance to both ancient Greek myths and modern life, but all I can think above the noise is that if sugar did the same thing to adults as it did to kids it would be worth fifty quid a gram.

Just when I get near the end I feel someone looking at me. I look up and a hunched, skinny man is standing not five feet from where I'm sat. He looks kind of ill in the way that long-time alkies sometimes get. The lines under his eyes make it look like someone has carved out chunks of his face, and despite the sun he's wearing a red hood up underneath his brown jacket.

My blessings to you, the man says. You got any spare change?

I'm thinking: Jesus, you can't go five minutes in this park without some failure asking you for skag money.

I'm saying: Sorry mate, it's almost the end of the month and I just spent the last of my coin.

The man nods once slowly.

I try not to stare. I can't work out the man's accent, nor the beat of his speech. And it looks like the man's skin should be olive coloured, but someone forgot to give him the correct dose of melanin.

Please, I live here in the park, the man says. I am waiting on a list for a flat. They say I am high priority and ask do I have a place to stay and I say yes but it does not happen and I am still in the park.

I'm thinking: At least he isn't coming out with his girlfriend is about to give birth and he needs 40p for the train to get to the hospital like the rest of them do.

I'm saying: That sounds like an adventure.

The man looks down at the grass for a second. No no, he says. I sleep with a big stick. A very very big stick. The trees make many noises, and I am always thinking it is a molester or a bear or a molester bear.

I shrug and hope the man gets the hint. I open up the book. I've only got a few days to skim it so I can impress Erin at Food Not Bombs on Friday.

You are reading? the man says.

I'm thinking: Not that it's any of your business, but it's just as well that I've not long looked through that review.

I'm saying: A book. Kate Tempest's *Brand New Ancients*. It's, like, the most relevant poems of the twenty-first century.

The man purses one eye. Relevant, he says. What is this word?

I'm thinking: I am not a walking dictionary.

I'm saying: It means, like, it's true about modern life.

2

The man stares back and I can't quite work out if he's one of those guys who suffer from resting pout face.

The man says, But that is not what is poetry. You can read Kahlil Gibran or Shakespeare and if it is poetry it is relevant. Even if it is from a long time ago.

I'm thinking: That's it, any money that I might have thought about giving to you or a homeless shelter on your behalf will now be donated to UKIP.

I'm saying: You seem very knowledgeable for someone who sleeps with a stick.

I am reading always, the man answers. In Central Library it is warm like the park today. And I am writing poetry always. They call me the Pavement Poet. My friend even has made me a Facebook page. Look, I am making a new one today.

The man points to one of the stones in the circle. It's one of the smaller ones that wouldn't even come up to my chest. I can make out a few lines written out in chalk. Every couple of letters, the text turns from blue to yellow to pink. It says:

* * *

When
    Something bad happen
It is always there
    When you close your eyes.

* * *

I rub my chin like it looks like I care. The man says, Do you like?

I'm thinking: This isn't even a pavement. We're in a stone circle. In a city park. And let's not get started on that typo.

I'm saying: Let's hope for your sake it doesn't rain tonight.

I check my phone to signal the end of the conversation. I have a message from Erin, informing me that a halloumi slammer is about as non-vegan as Donald Trump is non-fascist, and I decide that all these distractions are stopping me from being my best self.

I nod at the man, put the book in my satchel and walk away. I wonder if writing, 'Yes, that's the joke' to start my next message to Erin would help me save face. But then I hear a shout above the noise of the kids as I walk off.

Hey man, the man says, but I keep walking.

Man, listen, the man says again.

I feel a hand on my shoulder and I swing round.

I'm thinking: Leave me the hell alone. God, why can't you just go and overdose in a blocked-up gutter and drown?

I'm saying: Alright, mate, how can I help?

The man holds out something in his palm and says, Man, you forget your phone.

* * *

The next day is Thursday, and I go out for food with Tom. He insists on going to this cool new place on the edge of town called the Old Bus Station. I've been to places like this before. The Old Bus Station is an authentic, Shoreditch-style pop-up street food eaterie with authentic, Shoreditch-style vintage upcycled fittings and authentic, Shoreditch-style inflated rip-off prices. For the amount Tom paid for his third-wave Marxist pulled pork slaw bomb, he could have flown to a Samsung factory-town in Henan Province and convinced the family of a small boy to part with a transplant-ready kidney. In the corner, being watched by a bunch of people sat on old grammar school desk chairs and benches made of pallets, is one of those

4

guitar/keyboard bands that hunch over their instruments as if they're a bit apologetic about getting up on stage to express themselves. Tom says, What you having, mate?

I'm thinking: Craft beer names are getting more and more ridiculous by the second. I swear I just heard someone ask for two Starved Interns and a Paedo Biscuit.

I'm saying: I'll have a bottle of Liberal Tears. I'll be back in a sec, just gonna try and find some signal.

As I walk through the exhibition space at the back, I think that the more art shows I see, the more I want to stick a piece of wood to a loaf of bread and join in. I nod at the big doorman – the one with the shiny gold tooth and the SIA licence strapped tight around his arm – as the cold outside air hits me. My phone has one bar of 4G, which is just enough to tell Erin how much I'm looking forward to seeing her at Food Not Bombs tomorrow lunchtime. But then I hear a voice say, Hey man, you got any spare change?

I look over, and the Pavement Poet is kneeling in front of me, back to the wall, hood up and chalk in hand, finishing off a mural.

I'm thinking: I bet he can see up every girl's skirt from down there. He should change his name to the Pavement Pervert.

I'm saying: I don't, sorry. I just spent the last of my money at the bar.

I hit send. The Pavement Poet says, Man, do I know you?

I'm thinking: I wish Tom agreed to my suggestion of a few pints down the Lamb & Flag and a half 'n' half from Abrakebabra.

I'm saying: I don't think so, sorry mate. I doubt we mix in the same circles.

The Pavement Poet says, Now I know. We met this other day in the park. You are reading the book of relevant poetry and I tell you about Kahlil Gibran and Shakespeare. Look, I have a new poem. Do you like?

I look at the mural, all pink and yellow and blue. It says:

* * *

> If you love,
> love.
> If you hate,
> love.
> If you live,
> love.

* * *

I'm thinking: I've seen my angsty fifteen-year-old cousin share better motivational quotes on Instagram.

I'm saying: To be honest, I have actually seen worse at the Tate.

Before the Pavement Poet can reply, Tom pops his head out through the draught flaps. I'm short at the bar, he says. Chuck me a pound please, mate.

I flip over a coin and Tom catches it in his fist. I put my phone in my back pocket and make to go back inside, but the Pavement Poet says, Hey, you sure you got no change my man?

I'm thinking: I hate it when tramps catch you out like that.

I'm saying: Sorry, mate.

The Pavement Poet says, OK, man. I know how it is. The street food people are good. They will give me something later.

I'm thinking: So basically they give the tramps free food, but when I bought that chai crème brûlée earlier I almost had to cash in an ISA.

I'm saying: So you're saying I'm not a good person?

No no, the Pavement Poet says. I am saying the street food people give food. What is left is give to the poor, like the Sikh temple.

I'm thinking: I hope that ginger-dreaded trustafarian on the vegan pie stall who was coughing into his hands gives you his hippie-AIDS.

I'm saying: You do that. Wait for the street food people. But you should wait somewhere else. People don't like being harangued when they're trying to have a good time.

The doorman with the gold tooth comes out. You OK there, bro? He says. This guy ain't botherin you, is he?

I'm thinking: Now I've got you, 'man'. As soon as my new friend kicks you down the street I'm gonna piss all over your stupid little poem.

I'm saying: He's twenty-past-eleven drunk at twenty-past-eight. You know how aggro they get when they've had too much trampagne.

The doorman flexes his arms as he grabs the Pavement Poet by the scruff of his neck. It looks like the SIA licence is about to ping off. The Pavement Poet shouts and protests while he's being shoved down the street, and I scrape my foot over the half-finished mural and walk back inside.

* * *

Friday is a nice sunny day and I feel quite guilty for enjoying all the global warming. I walk past the lunchtime drinkers enjoying their smokes in the sun and spot the Food Not Bombs stall. By the looks of the different coloured poles and the masking tape holding it together at the seams, it looks about time that they took a new abandoned gazebo when they're next at a festival. It's plastered in typical anti-capitalist/anarchist slogans: Smash the Fash. Viva la Podemos. Jeremy Corbyn for Proportionally Representative Community Leader. I spot Erin handing a guy some plates from a battered shopping trolley and think that there's something about dreads and jeggings that makes me want to growl.

I get all the shrapnel from my pocket and pick out the coppers to donate. It's almost two o'clock and some of the lunchtime drinkers are queuing, along with a few curious shoppers and a lady in her Poundland uniform. But I don't pay them much attention as I'm too busy staring at Erin.

I get to the front of the queue. Oh, hey, Erin says. Come around this side so we can have a chat.

She gives my arm a squeeze and I'm disappointed not to get a hug. Erin talks about how the good weather has made Food Not Bombs busier than normal, and then I say, I read that book you lent me. The Kate Tempest one.

Oh yeah, Erin says. What did you think?

I'm thinking: This is where I impress her with my amazing analytical skills.

I'm saying: It's a great book. The album version is fantastic too. I suppose you could say that it's a highly relevant piece of work for the world we live in now. But then again, poetry should always be relevant. You could read Carl Gibran or Shakespeare and if it's true poetry it will always be relevant.

Erin says, I think you mean *Kahlil* Gibran. We did him in second year.

I'm thinking: For fuck's sake, I should have YouTube'd him.

I'm saying: It just came out of my mouth weird.

I was reintroduced to him recently by this poet from that part of the world, she says. He has the most amazing story. I even set him up a Facebook page.

I'm thinking: Oh my dear lord it cannot be oh bugger bugger bugger.

8

I'm saying: No kidding.

Erin looks over my shoulder. There he is. Tariq, she says. As-Salaam-Alaikum.

And I hear someone say, Wa-Alaikum-Salaam.

I look round. Sat on the floor behind me, chalk in hand, is the Pavement Poet.

I'm thinking: This is almost as bad as when Tesco ran out of Mother's Day flowers and I had to give my mum a bouquet of bananas.

I'm saying: Oh great, I like a bit of art.

The text itself is in pink and yellow, and I wonder why he didn't buy more blue after the Old Bus Station. The poem reads:

* * *

Now I know
how to swim
is relevant.
Now I know
what is brave
is relevant.
Now I know
what is regret
is relevant.

* * *

See? Erin says. It's enough to break your heart. I just want to go somewhere quiet and cry right now.

I'm thinking: You're not the only one.

I'm saying: I like words. Aren't words the best?

He's from Damascus, originally, Erin says. He escaped

9

during the insurgency. You should ask him about his three-day journey to Europe on the boat from Benghazi to Lampedusa with all the Eritreans, or about being strapped to the underside of a lorry by his belt for seventeen hours coming over from Calais.

I'm thinking: I desperately need to get out of this situation, but all that's going through my head is that life under the sea is better than anything they got up there.

I'm saying: I bet that was one hell of an adventure. Did you see Strictly last week? I swear Bruno fancies Peter Andre.

But Erin just acts like I never said anything. She says, It should have been a great day when he got his papers. But they literally give you three weeks' notice to leave the centre and the support just isn't there anymore. So, Jolyon, meet Tariq, the Pavement Poet. Tariq, this is Jolyon.

As he turns to look at me, I realise how still Tariq has been while Erin was speaking.

I'm thinking: Maybe he won't recognise me again. Could I pretend to be Australian? Or Swiss? Would Erin notice if I faced away from her when I talk?

I'm saying: Pleased to meet you, fella.

You don't have to tell me about that man, Tariq says. That is the man about who I am telling you.

What? That can't be right, Erin says, unsure of who she's talking to. This must be some kind of mistake.

Tariq puts down his yellow chalk and picks up the pink one and says, I tell him about Kahlil Gibran and Shakespeare and how poetry is always relevant but he wishes me away with his words. I am telling you that I am knowing this man of the last week and he is the worst of the universe. Oh, holy.

Erin looks at me and says, But that's what you just said.

I'm thinking: It's OK, it's OK, she still thinks you're a

charming young gentleman as you've yet to ask for a naked selfie.

I'm saying: It's not quite how he says it. He's been pestering me wherever I go.

I hardly think that's true, Erin says. I have to admit that I've always found you to be a bit of a creep, Jolyon. Keep the book. You need as much poetry in your life as you can get.

And Tariq says, I got nothing to say to you, my man.

Tariq gets to putting another layer of chalk over his poem so it won't rub out, and Erin turns to the next person in the queue and asks them if they want the lentil dhal or the spring vegetable stew. For the first time in my life I feel how alone I am. It's as if I'm watching the world through the portal of my stained glass eyes from somewhere far inside my own head, as if I'm stood still and unclothed and being hailed on by spits and stones of sulphuric ash.

I'm thinking:

I'm saying:

The Tea Party

She could feel it in the way that Kieron holds the cwtchy part at the back of her neck as they kiss, the way they sync together on the bed. She on the right, he on the left, as if these had always been their sides and she had known him all her life. But as he slinks his arm over her shoulder to hold her closer, Nana walks into Danielle's room without knocking again. She's holding another two mugs of sweet tea. Danielle looks at Kieron as he presses pause on his phone and she says, told you so. It wasn't as if this was the first time, nor as if it would be the last.

They watch Nana walk to the bookcase in the corner of the room, dragging the soles of her pink slippers as she moves. Between the dim light of the bedside lamp and the television, her skin looks so dark it's as if she had never left the island. She avoids the clothes and the ashtray on the floor, and puts the mugs of tea down on top of Danielle's to-be-read pile. Danielle thinks how if the mess in her room wasn't in the exact places it's been in for the last six years, Nana would probably end up on the floor.

We just thought you would both want maybe a nice cup of tea, she says, as she dries her hands in her apron. And you can have some nice ginger loaf as well, if you want a slice.

Nana pays no attention to the tea she made fifteen minutes ago, on top of the chest of drawers in pale blue mugs. Danielle gets up and takes the mugs off the book pile and puts them next to the ones on the chest to make a point. But Nana doesn't even notice. She just smiles while looking at Danielle as if nothing else matters. The same smile Nana would give when she was trying to comfort her after the break up with Milan. The only difference Danielle can notice in her smile between then and now is that she's had six years more tea, so the shine is going from her gold fang.

Alright, Nana, Danielle says. We don't want nothin at the moment, thank you. We just wants to be left alone for a bit. If we does want somethin, I'll come down and find you.

Kieron waits until Nana is out of earshot before giving his apology. Sorry, love, he says, as he looks at the foot of the bed. Another cuppa and it'll mess up my sleepin pattern, like.

Danielle nests herself down on the bed, and puts her arm between his back and the pillow. She wished he could understand. He was starting five straight night shifts tomorrow so they wouldn't even get to see each other until after he'd had Michaela for the weekend. He only got her once every two weeks so it wasn't as if he could cancel.

Kieron presses play on his phone, and on the telly the type-A ad executive mother leans in to kiss the adorkable scientist love interest just as her jealous stoner son plonks himself between them with a plate of tacos and asks if this is a bad time. Danielle's arm is getting sore, so she pulls it out from underneath him and they kiss, and she doesn't even pull away, even though he hasn't had a shave for three days and it feels like she's brushing against a small cactus. Just as her other hand reaches his waist, she hears the carpet bristle against the door, and she turns around to see the bobbing white head of Nana entering the room again. Danielle figures that she couldn't have left the landing.

We were just wondrin, Nana says, as she takes a few steps past an empty wine bottle, if you want some ginger loaf. We gonna have one downstairs. We can't remember the answer.

The wrinkles on her face start to make sense when she smiles.

Danielle holds her head in her hand. She tries to count her breaths. Nana, she says. Listen. Can you please just GO AWAY. Leave us alone, for Christ's sake.

Nana blinks once as her eyebrows go up. She opens her mouth, then after a second she says, We just tryna bein nice, Dani.

For crying out loud, Danielle says. Stop all this bloody 'We' business and all. Grancha is dead. He's been dead bloody years. Get a grip, you daft bat.

Nana pants a breath out, and snaps the same air back in. Now, there no need for that, she says.

Danielle knew this. She thought of how much easier it was when Aunty Ameena and Tia Maria were still alive. Before Mrs Mullaghan went to the home. She would never forget the tea parties Nana used to have. When Danielle was a child, they would almost always run out of ginger loaf, and when Nana went into the kitchen to get another, Tia Maria would go into her long red purse and get out a 50p coin. And then Aunty Ameena would smile and shake her head and press another into Danielle's hands, and the two ladies would look at Mrs Mullaghan and she would tut first and then get out her purse, and she would say there ye are little one and pass over another 50p, even though she rarely spoke and always frowned at kids.

But this wasn't a tea party. This was meant to be her alone time with Kieron finally. So she said, Please, Nana, just leave us alone. You can be such a bloody pain.

Nana's head goes down, unwilling and unable to meet Danielle's eyes. She turns on the spot, rocking from foot to foot. When she turns to shut the door, Danielle can see that her right hand is up near her throat.

No word is spoken. All Danielle can think of is how she should have moved out by now, how she should have made more of an effort to meet people after Milan, instead of falling into a routine with Nana and thinking that everyone who showed any interest in her was just gonna split her heart in two once more. She doesn't stop wishing she could just fall asleep and wake up six years ago until Kieron speaks.

I think you should apologise, he says. She's just tryina be nice.

For half a moment, Danielle tenses her neck. Don't take her side, she says. You dunno what it's like. Nana's been doin this for six years. If I'm in the house then she don't leave me alone.

Let's go spend some time with her, Kieron tries again. I can set it all up on the downstairs telly.

No, she says, and she takes her hand off his lap. She wants to say that the whole point of them being up in her room was so they didn't have to spend time with Nana, and instead spend time with each other. Nana would talk over the telly and make sweet tea every ten minutes and tut at all the swearing. But while she's thinking of a way to tell him, Kieron says, I'm not pressin play until you goes down and says sorry.

Danielle shakes her head and gets up. They stay silent as the carpet bristles when she opens the door. She wishes she knew how to make him understand without mentioning Milan, but all she can do is put her hand on the small of his back as they walk out the room.

They go down the stairs in time to hear the kettle boil. They walk through the hall and open the kitchen door. Danielle hears the kettle click on the counter. It is only then that she sees Nana in the middle of the floor, spread out across the tiles.

Danielle feels like she's watching herself from the corner of the room. What you doin on the floor, she says. Get up from there, you daft bat.

Since they last saw her, a few minutes before, Nana's skin has gone from its normal capuccino colour to an almost pavement grey. Her head is turned to the side and there's blood running from her nose, all the way to the floor.

Stop messin around, Danielle says, while pursing her eyes into two paper slits. Get up now, Nana.

Kieron strides across the kitchen. Can you hear me, Mrs Oliveira? he says. Are you there?

Danielle leans over from the door. She can't go any closer, even if she wanted to.

She ain't breathin, Kieron says, and his mouth starts trembling in time with his hands.

As Kieron moves Nana onto her back, Danielle can see that Nana's arms and legs are as limp as the strands on the head of an old mop. Kieron tilts Nana's head back, but he can't seal his lips around the old dear's mouth without splashing her face with tears.

He starts to press down on Nana's chest. In the half-minute that he pushes up and down on her sternum, Danielle feels like she's being coated from the inside with lead paint. She goes to move, to do anything, then realises that there's nothing for her to do. She stands there, looking at Nana on the floor, draped as if someone has just pushed a dull dishcloth off the kitchen side.

Nana just needs a cup of tea, she says eventually. She sinks cups of sweet tea like I used to sink bottles of prosecco. I'll make us all a round.

She flicks the kettle back on and waits for the click. As she puts the tea bags into three pale blue mugs, Kieron looks up after puffing into Nana's mouth.

What the hell are you doin? he says. Call an ambulance, for Christ's sake.

Danielle goes out to the garden, makes the phone call, and

tries to light a cigarette. She can see into the kitchen, but she can't see Nana and Kieron on the kitchen floor. By the time she's managed to work the lighter's flint, she notices that Kieron is standing up and screaming at her through the window to answer the doorbell.

The paramedics go through to the kitchen, and the younger one takes the defibrillator off his shoulder and uses the strap to rest it on the floor next to Nana. Danielle goes back into the garden and picks up her cigarette, almost out. She sucks it back to life, just as Kieron comes through and tells her to get in the ambulance. A paramedic follows. The older, balder one. He pats Kieron on the shoulder and tells him what a good job he's done. Kieron tells him that the first aid course he did was the only one the Jobcentre sent him on that was worth going to.

What's your name? The paramedic says to Danielle. But Danielle can't even look him in the face.

* * *

On West 3, in the far corner, the nasogastric tube leaves Nana's nose at the tip. The purple bruises where she fell mean that they couldn't even stick the tube down to the side of her face. Danielle wishes Kieron wasn't working so she had someone to talk to every time Nana shut her eyes.

Nana breathes in, and fills the top third of her lungs.

Danielle wants to tell her that she shouldn't have shouted, and that she likes it that she gets mugs of sweet tea from her. She loves it that she gets tuna mayo sandwiches and a hot flask of tea made every morning before she goes off to the market.

But there's nothing she can do except hold the warm leather of Nana's hand.

17

Nothing she can do but smooth the spare skin around her wrist.

Nothing she can do but watch her, as Nana looks out the window at the allotments on the other side of the dual carriageway, packed with that ferocious August green. As Danielle follows her eyes, she stops paying attention to what Nana is watching. Instead she notices the way that she looks at it all. She is looking with the sunken, crow-pecked eyes of an abandoned lamb. Seeing everything as if for the first time, or maybe as if for the last.

She manages to roll her neck back, and looks up at the pale, diluted sky outside. Looking down at their locked hands, Danielle notices the tone of Nana's skin is still not back to the light brown of her own.

I'll be OK, Nana says, to no one in particular. And the tube from her nose, it grows a little longer.

* * *

When Kieron gets to the hospital, they go outside to the park to share a cigarette. Danielle wasn't even sure Nana knew they were leaving.

They sit down on the bench, looking at the row of shrubs. Kieron passes Danielle half a lit cigarette. Danielle passes over half a cup of sweet tea in a polystyrene cup. Kieron accepts, and while holding the cup with both hands, he takes a little sip. I dunno if she'll ever leave that ward, he says.

Danielle tries to open her mouth to speak, but fumbles the filter up to her lips instead. She takes a long drag. Kieron gives her the cup back and she takes another sip. As she does so she realises that soon there will be no Nana to wake her up with a mug of tea each morning. No Nana to have fish and chips with when Kieron is on a night shift. She remembers when it was the other way round, when she had come to stay with Nana after her break up with Milan. Nana would be the one to bring her tea and make sure she got out of bed, but somewhere in the last six years, Danielle had started being the one to peel back the covers for Nana to gently swing her legs round, or even to bring a bowl of hot water and a flannel to her bedroom so she could wash.

She doesn't breathe in again until she has to. Until she knows she can speak without crying. She says it quickly, before she has a chance to think about the words coming out of her own mouth. When I held her hand in there, she says, that was the first time I'd touched her because I hadn't wanted to in six years.

They both let their heads hang. Danielle closes her eyes.

Kieron takes the cigarette out of her hands, takes the last drag, and lets it drop on the floor. I'll tell you one thing I know, he says. The people we love never really leave us. Sometimes, even when they're not around any more, we still keep them alive in other ways.

Danielle picks up the butt. She looks past the concourse and up towards the vast grey hospital block itself, and tries to guess which window is the one next to Nana. She thinks about how easy it would have been just to put another two mugs of sweet tea down on her bookcase and say yes to a slice of ginger loaf.

Nana will always be with me, she says, and she turns to face Kieron. Do you want a cup of tea? I don't know why but I could really do with another cup of sweet tea right now. And maybe a piece of ginger loaf, too.

The Anatomy of a Beating

Here's a few words that will help you understand more about the world and your place in it than anything you've ever heard before:

In life, violence solves everything.

That's the way it's always been. The guy who attacks first and smashes hardest always wins. The caveman spends all day pulling down trees for a field and a fire and a bigger caveman gives him a slap. Then the bigger caveman's got his field and his wood and another caveman comes along and tonks him with a stick. Then another one comes along and tonks the tonker with an axe.

Before you know it everyone is tonking everyone. The guy who's done the most tonking has got himself a country and an army and the right to tonk anyone's swede he likes, cos he got a crown on his own.

Just think about it for a second. There would be nothing wrong in being a sheep if there weren't so many wolves herding you in the wrong direction. If you have a problem, you only need to know one thing: the trick to getting what you want in life is to hit the other guy harder, faster and more times than he hits you.

Don't believe me? Get this.

It's chest and triceps day. There ain't nothing better than a good session on a rusty bar. You knows you had a good workout when you looks down at your palms and it looks like you been slathering yourself in fake tan. After smashing it down the gym, I takes my usual shortcut back through the park. Sat on the altar in the middle of the stone circle is the usual mixture of moshers and alkies, enjoying the first bit of warm Easter weather. It's one of those times of the day when my abs disappear under the swell from being twelve hundred calories heavier post-workout. But I can still get away with a size small T-shirt, as long as I breathes in.

The group measures about twenty people, aged from about fifteen for the moshers to about forty for the alkies. I'm downwind and the smoke hangs low in the air stinging my nose like a freshly-cut hedge. It can only mean one thing. Some twonkey has been daft enough to beat me to the business. I won't sell anything I have in my back pocket, which means no glutamine for after tomorrow's back and biceps session.

And then I sees him. Propped on one elbow on the floor with his hood up by them, I sees this fatso endomorph I knows called Gordo. He pretends he's thick as his nana's gravy but like most people, if he didn't get so off it on booze and smoke all the time then he'd have a bit of substance to his swede.

He's got all the endo traits. Big bones, wide waist, fat arse. He must be six foot one and twenty stone eight, give or take half a pound. He looks so unhealthy that his face is almost as red as the hoodie he's wearing.

So anyways, I walks up to Gordo and even though we ain't yet made eye contact, we both knows each other is there. 'Sapnin brer,' I goes to him. 'Long time.'

He stays propped up on his elbow, one knee in the air. 'Safe,' he goes. 'Ain't seen you in time, bro.'

I'm talking as I walks behind him slowly, pretending I'm looking at the castle. There's nothing more satisfying than standing in front of a bloated future cancer victim, knowing that you will never be like that. Nothing better than being at the top while staring down at the bottom of the sexual food chain.

'Just chillin, is it?' I goes to him.

'I signs on in half-hour.'

'Is it,' I goes. 'No one can survive on what they chucks at you.'

Gordo's problems are two-fold: he's fat, and he's on the one-ply bog roll side of poor. His life could only get worse if he woke up ginger.

'They does it on purpose, spar. It don't make ends meet at all. I even got my Mumma to sign a form saying she's my landlady so I gets housin benefit. But it still ain't even enough to make a decent wedge. They taxes people so much they could give you double what they does, easy.'

I starts to wonder why he even needs to stop me getting glutamine if he has a two-way raise. He can't be on the bag, so it must be for all the junk that goes to baste all his organs.

'You got a cheek, brer,' I goes. 'You never paid a tax in your life unless you count the VAT on all the chocolate you buys. I bet your fags are from Poland and your booze is from France.'

Easy start, half a smile.

'Yeah, but it's still not enough money though, standard.'

'I knows you doesn't make enough to buy that new hoodie, brer. You musta been robbin your Mumma's tramadol again.'

'We've all got a raise,' he goes, trying to be clever. 'Can't go through life without a raise or two.'

When someone tries to be clever at your expense, it ain't half gonna go towards spoiling your day.

'Is it fuck,' I goes. 'All you knows about life is bein fat.'

He props his swede under his chins, and gives me a look like someone just spread dogshit over his top lip.

'Calm down, princess. I'm just sayin that we all got to do what we all got to do.'

22

I kicks the bottom of his shoe a few times. Not too hard, just enough to make him limp when he walks next. His face scrunches up so much, it might as well have fallen into a black hole. 'Let's be honest, Gord,' I goes, and he shakes his foot out as he winces from the pain. 'I can see what everyone down here is up to. I knows what your raise involves, and it's pissin all over my raise.'

My mouth must have been frothing a bit by now, cos I notice in my peripherals that most of the moshers and alkies on the rocks have turned to face the other way.

'Stay back,' Gordo goes, fingers out in front his outstretched arms. 'I knows people who knows people.'

I give him a few more kicks on his legs. As the fourth or fifth punt connects I hears a voice behind me.

'Just what do you think you're doing?' some guy goes.

I turns around and it's an almost classic ectomorph standing there, one of the alkies who was sat on the rocks. Five foot ten, seventy-two inch reach and a whole ten stone five. Long, thin limbs, and more fat in a glass of skimmed milk than there is on his waist. He's got the round sloping shoulders of a guy who couldn't press a bag of sugar. As he tries to out-stare me, I notice that the arms of his T-shirt are flapping in the slight breeze. I can never understand why people think it's OK to go through life so underdeveloped. As if they think that no one is going to notice. This knob-end doesn't even realise that there ain't no point even buying T-shirts unless they looks sprayed on. And if you ain't got the shoulders to wear them like that, then you shouldn't even be alive.

I could just not answer. Sooner or later, he'd realise that he might as well have soaked himself in petrol and asked for a light. But I doesn't want him to know that yet.

So I goes, 'Sapnin, brer. Gorra dog?'

I points my finger at him but make sure that it's lower than head height. This makes him want to give me an answer, even though he doesn't know it.

'What? No,' he goes, and he don't even clock that I've stepped over Gordo and taken three steps towards him. 'I mean, my mother has.'

'Standard,' I goes, taking another three slow steps. 'What breed then? I bet it's a *bichon frise*. All women loves a fluffy clean *bichon frise*.'

'Uh, spaniel,' he says, still not noticing as I step forward again to make it six feet between us now.

I brings my hand up to my ear and pretends I can't really hear him. Another step and he is within my reach. 'Well worrisit then? Don't leave me guessin. A bitch?'

He's standing head on with all the prime targets down the middle of his body showing. The nose, the jaw, the solar plexus, the balls. I'm stood three-quarters on, chin down.

'No, it's a boy.'

He's so comfy now that he doesn't even realise that my right heel has come up off the ground. He wouldn't even have noticed this if his name was Bruce Lee.

'Ah, worra pity,' I answers back. 'My dog wants a shag.'

And before he's even had a chance to digest what I just said, I twists and exhales and throws forward a fist. I tenses every muscle in my body on the moment of impact, which puts my front two knuckles forward an extra half-inch.

His jaw crumples back like an empty can of beer. On his way down his arms come out forward for protection but they are one-tenth of a second too late. They stays up even when his swede and the rest of his body has tonked on the ground.

That's the most satisfying sound to any ears. That moment when the head smashes against the floor like someone has dropped a box of eggs. It's the sound of him half-remembering all the time he spent learning karate in the community hall when he was a nipper. All the taekwondo he learnt after school. All the wing chun in college. It's the sound of him realising that all that martial farts training meant fuck all outside the Dojo.

We're all cavemen, after all. So we might as well act like them.

So I turns round and Gordo hasn't moved. He's looking at his mate and when his mate's hands go down, Gordo flinches. He knows he best not go help. Then I leans over the guy and I puts my finger in his face.

'Fuck you and your eleven inch arms,' I goes. 'You're a smelly fuckin binrat who should mind his own business. Now go eat a fuckin pie.'

Just then, I looks up and I sees a reflective vest and a pair of shiny shoes walking towards us, about forty yards away. It's a Plod walking over from the west gate of the park, the town end. He must be taking a short cut back to Central which is just the other side of the trees.

I make a quick calculation. If I fucks off now the other way to where he's going, he'll bell Central and they'll be at the other end of the park before I gets to the east gate. I'll be in a cell overnight, and they'll only feed me fibre-less junk that weighs in at about four hundred calories. I'll wake up tomorrow with loose skin where everything has deflated. And if I tries to run past him, he'll get out his truncheon and tonk me like I was a caveman with a fire and a field.

Quick as I can, I gets on my knees and puts my ear to the cripple's mouth. I slips my wraps under his back. I lose five twenty-bags, wrapped in greaseproof paper so my prints don't stick, some ephedrine, and seven wraps of GHB. This kills my post-training recovery plans. I makes a mental note to bill the cripple on the floor when he gets out of court.

When plod gets a bit closer, I gets to clock him a bit better.

He's wearing a reflective jacket but his eyes are wide open and his cheeks are sucked in, so he must be a PCSO. The only real weapon they carries is a radio. He must be five foot eleven, twelve stone two and all of about twenty-one years old. The stab vest and flat hat make it impossible to tell if he's endo or meso, but if he was as gorgeous as me underneath all that gear then he'd look fat right now. That's easily enough a good reason to make anyone not want to be a copper.

I waits for Plod to speak before I decides what to do. Best let them think they're leading the conversation, even if he is the youngest person present by a few years.

'Alright then,' he goes. 'What's going on here? No bollocks now, or you're all in trouble.'

His radio is up by his cheek, eyes over all of us.

Gordo does the right thing and keeps his gums from flapping. 'I'm a personal trainer, Officer,' I goes. 'My client and I were just off on a jog and we noticed this poor guy in a bit of distress. I think it may have been an attempted robbery. It's dangerous around here.'

'Really,' he goes. He speaks into his radio, requesting back up and an ambulance. 'Stand back, mate. I'm just going to check him out.'

It can only be a few seconds before the wannabe copper discovers the haul underneath the cripple so I decides it's about time to go. 'Get up now, Gord,' I goes. 'You've had enough of a rest. You'll achieve nothing there on the floor.'

Gordo is up and high-kneeing it away faster than I ever thought he could move, heading to the Town entrance of the park where Plod just came from. I'm quite disappointed that he isn't limping a bit more.

'Mate,' the copper shouts as I chase Gordo down. 'Stay right there. We're going to need a statement.'

I'm cupping my hand to my ear as I legs it off, knowing

that the PCSO won't go far when there's an injured guy out sparko. 'Yeah, cool,' I goes. 'But not on my client's time. A few more laps, a few more press-ups and we'll be down the station, standard.'

Soon as you know it, we're out through the castle gates and lost in the drum of motors and feet. I waits for Gordo to catch up with me and I tells him to sit on the floor. He collapses and his gut goes up and down where he's breathing. He takes up so much room on the pavement that people have to go on the road to walk past him.

'You grass me up and you're bitin the kerb,' I goes, pointing down at him. 'Ain't my fault your spar got a big mouth.'

He don't answer back, cos he knows not to. Seeing him panting on the floor with his belly going up and down makes me want to smash my abs with some reverse crunches, even though I worked out earlier today.

I'm about to turn away and walk back to my yard when Gordo looks up at me. There ain't even no anger in his face. 'Why you always got to be this way?' he goes.

I feels like he just pushed the big red button on my forehead. I wants to leave a hollow where his face should be. I wants to lick his grey slimy brain guts off my fist. But instead I goes all soft and quiet and I goes, 'Cos violence solves everything in life, spar. I can show you if you wants.'

Gordo looks ahead and goes, 'But you wasn't violent to that cop and you got out of trouble there by learnin to fight another day.'

I wants to explode his nose all over my shirt. I wants to hit him till one of his four front teeth is sticking out my fist.

'You best stuff another cake in that fuckin hole of yours,' I goes, as I leans over him and brings my hand back.

'Why you think everyone only buys off me now?' he goes.

I wants to bring my boot back and punt his nasal bone into

27

his skull. I wants to catch his eyes with my heel and pop them over his face.

My hand drops. 'Cos you stole all my customers.'

'It's cos they can't be arsed with the grief that comes from buyin off you. You're too unpredictable.'

I wants to smash him till I has to catch my breath, then I wants to stop for a second to listen to his swallowing as two pints of blood tries to make its way down his throat. I brings my fist back again and Gordo looks up at me, and his face is saying, go on, prove me right.

And then it comes to me. I expects to feel something, or maybe even anything, but there's nothing there. The moment when I'm getting what I wanted and I'm expecting to feel better. That horrible surprise waiting when you achieves your goal. And I hates myself even more when I finally admits that I knew it all along.

Violence don't solve everything. No matter how many times he gets hurt or how many teeth Gordo loses, he will always be right if I hits him even once.

I turns and walks over the bridge out of town, wondering what else I doesn't know about the world.

Untitled (Text on Paper, 2018)

Two more ticks on the clean-down checklist and she was done. Alexis picked up the bottle trolley and emptied it into the wheelie bin, careful to lean back when the bottles smashed so she didn't get covered in dregs. She pushed it through the beer garden, but when she got near the Dutch Trader back door, she heard the distinct sound of a clink. It was coming from the fire escape stairs, as if someone had just struck the metal railings.

She stood still. She didn't breathe. Then after a couple of seconds, she said, 'Who's there?'

No answer came. She wondered if it was one of the alley cats, or if one of the pisshead regulars had gone up there to see the city lights but had fallen asleep. She got her phone out of her apron and put on the flashlight. She held it up where she thought she heard the noise, and on the second landing she saw a man. The light was in his face, and he was holding up a wet brush so it wasn't shining in his eyes. He was wearing a blue woolly hat and fingerless gloves, and through the railings she could see a yellow bucket by his feet. Directly behind him was the picture of an ornate gilt frame with a blank space in the middle, still soaked from where he had just pasted it.

She hated how some of the dickheads that were hardcore into graff thought that the walls of the Dutch Trader were a free-for-all. It seemed like every dickhead out there was doing wanksy-style paste ups nowadays. The walls of the Dutch

Trader beer garden – both inside and out – were covered in them. And this guy staring down at her was the biggest dickhead of all.

Hugo Deri Jones. She could never forget that name. She had seen it come up so often on her Facebook feed that she had to mute him, even before they had met. Then, when they finally did meet at the Alderman Fellowship awards, he had asked her first where the toilets were, and then to get him a beer, as if she was some kind of gopher or assistant and not a fellow nominee.

'I know who you are, so if you jump over the wall now I won't call the police,' she said.

Hugo smirked at her and said, 'Ah, the perils of being Instagram famous.'

Typical, Alexis thought. He still doesn't know who I am. She was about to say that they had even had a photoshoot with the other awardees (where he had manoeuvred himself into the middle of every picture) but she stopped herself. Instead she said, 'Please, just go. I've got a big day tomorrow.'

'Give me five more minutes and I'm done. That's not too much to ask of a fan, is it?'

The light of the moon was weak. She wondered if he could see her rolling her eyes. 'If I was you,' she said, 'I wouldn't waste a single second more on it.'

He frowned and smiled at the same time. Then he said, 'I didn't know serving wenches knew much about art. I thought your specialist subjects were normally benefit fraud and having children with multiple fathers.'

He was such a tit. She couldn't wait to tell Emily. She swapped her phone from her left hand to her right, making sure that the light stayed on him. She said, 'You'd be surprised by what I know. And I know a crap piece of art when I see it.'

He smirked, and put his brush in the bucket. 'I doubt you'd understand. This is a hybrid piece. It's an immuno-collaborative post-particle reflection. It challenges the viewer to create their own art, yet it is tucked away in the most inaccessible of places.'

'It's a bit of white wallpaper with a border to make it look like it's been framed,' Alexis said. 'I've seen my six-year-old cousin do better work in Spoons with three Crayolas and a beer mat.'

Hugo's smile was still irritatingly smug. She wondered how long he was going to hold that face, and got ready to pick up an ashtray off the nearest picnic bench in case he came down the stairs. He said, 'Just as I thought. Not everyone "gets" art.'

She smirked back at him and said, 'You literally just said a bunch of random words. Tell me what an immuno-collaborative post-particle reflection is.'

He said nothing.

She looked behind him, taking in the work again. She shook her head and said, 'It's a shit piece of art. You're no Blek le Rat when it comes to street art, are you? And no Rachel Whiteread when it comes to neo-conceptualism. This kind of stuff will be thought of as an embarrassment to both movements in ten years, and I hope you and your shit art, for keeping me stood here in the cold when I just wanna go home and sleep, both die a fucking death.'

He kept on staring. She could see the anger rise inside him. His face went red, and she could practically feel his heart thumping as the pressure of the blood and cortisol brought his veins to the surface of his temples. Then he calmed and flashed his eyes down before looking back at her, and she realised that she'd hurt him. She remembered back to the award ceremony, when everyone, Emily included, was talking to him as if he was a god. But Alexis had never had time for this type of art, or for showoffs like Hugo. He had no idea what this picture meant or what it actually was, and the first person to see it had called him out on it.

'I'm done,' he said. 'I don't have to stay here and listen to this.'

She turned the light off her phone. She put it back in her apron, and put the Dutch Trader keys in her hand and made a fist so there was a key between each finger. But he hooked the bucket over his shoulder and walked along the fire escape landing until he was next to the wall. Then he put his body through the rail so he could climb down it. Alexis crossed her arms expectantly. Then before she could move, he took the brush out of the bucket and swung it hard, emptying it in her direction. She saw the paste come up towards her, and she tried to get out of its way but it caught her on the side of her face. She felt the coldness of it seep through her shirt. She looked up, but all she caught was his head disappearing over the wall, then she heard him run off down the alley.

She wanted to jump over the wall. She wanted to chase him down and batter the back of his head with a bottle. But instead she wiped the paste out of her eyes so she could see. When she was back inside the Dutch Trader with the door locked she found some blue roll behind the bar and cleaned herself down as best as she could. It was a cold night, and the paste made it worse, and she didn't take her hood off until she was back home.

* * *

She arrived the next day at the Nos Dada at eight, and it was already as full as she'd ever seen it at any other group show opening. Previously, when she had turned up late after a few drinks, the place would be so packed that she wouldn't even bother going in. Instead she would stay outside to talk to the other artists she knew, while drinking from the bladder of wine she brought in her bag, until Emily led everyone to her local. But this time one of her pictures was in the show, and she wouldn't have stayed outside if you wanted to pay her.

She walked up the stairs to the first floor, and saw her picture on the whitewashed back wall. She was pleased Emily had put it there, rather than at the top of the stairs, as it would be one of the first things people would notice as they looked down the long hall of the attic. She made her way towards it, squeezing past people holding plastic cups of wine and talking in small groups. There was a sizeable number looking at her picture: the azures and opals she had put into the ocean, which she balanced out with the orange of the setting sun catching the watching men waiting for the waves, were caught well under the sympathetic spotlight. Emily and the crew had done a good job.

She saw a woman with henna hair in a cherry red poncho standing in front of her picture. It felt to Alexis that the woman was not only taking the picture in, but trying to notice how everyone else was looking at it. Then the woman noticed Alexis looking, and Alexis realised that it was Emily. They hugged and Alexis said, 'I didn't recognise you for a second. I'm too used to seeing you in your dungarees and paint-spattered Docs.'

'Oh, you know, got to make the effort if the Arts Council are turning up,' Emily said. 'If you want to get funding from the Old White Men then you need to look the part.'

It was a strange thing for Emily, of all people, to say, Alexis thought. It didn't sound like the person she went to university with. But it was indicative of what had happened to the place. Emily started the Nos Dada because she never felt she had a chance in the art world. But as soon it got some success, she started attracting other types of artists who wanted to prove their authenticity by exhibiting there. By now it was a firmly established venue, both on the city's art scene and on the tourist trail along with the national museum and the more commercial galleries.

'You're hoping for funding?' Alexis said.

'Not for the Nos Dada, exactly. I've heard they're sending round selectors for the Biennale. Whoever they ask is going to need a curator with them,' she said, and she winked.

Alexis tried to think of something to say, but her mind was already racing. She had been to Venice as a student, to work as an invigilator in the Wales Pavilion. It meant that she maxed out her overdraft and had to work double shifts at the Dutch Trader for weeks after she came back, but she still remembered the chance to go round the other pavilions every day as the most inspirational summer of her life. And here Emily was, stood in front of her picture, waiting for the Arts Council's representative to turn up. She said, 'I didn't realise it was that time of year already.'

'Sure is. The Old White Men will be out in force. I have a feeling they'll be interested in this piece.'

Emily stepped to the side. Next to Alexis's painting was a sculpture she hadn't seen when she had come to the Nos Dada to drop off her work the week before: it was a mannequin wearing a suit, bent over with its backside in the air. Hundreds of twenty pound notes were held up behind it with fishing line, as if they'd just left its rear end. When Alexis looked closer, she noticed that the Queen had been replaced by Meghan Markle wearing a Margaret Thatcher wig. Dozens of people were around it taking pictures, or taking selfies as close to the mannequin as they could.

'It's great, isn't it?' Emily said.

Alexis felt her stomach drop. It wasn't so much that she'd got her hopes up for a second than that Emily thought the artist who'd made this monstrosity was someone she wanted to work with. She said, 'I don't think it's to my taste.'

Emily looked at it for a second, then said, 'Fair enough. This kind of thing is really hot right now.'

Alexis looked at it again, and then at the crowds of people taking selfies with it. She saw a man in a tartan jacket who was talking with his friend walk near. They stopped talking and laughed when they noticed it. She said, 'What do you like about it?'

Emily looked at her. 'I don't know. It just looks good, I suppose.'

'Then what does it mean?'

'I don't think art has to mean anything in particular. The correct question is normally not, *what does it mean*? But instead, *what is it*?'

Alexis looked at the sculpture. After a second she said, 'I could understand how that might work if we were looking at a Basquiat ripoff or a site-specific, Gallaccio-type installation, but when it's a man, with a woman's face coming out of him in this way, I think that this artist is trying to say something, and what he is trying to say is not good.'

Emily looked at the sculpture, then out of nowhere she laughed, and Alexis felt her face go red. She cursed herself for speaking out. She forgot that the curator has a personal attachment, an emotional responsibility even, to liking the work they choose to display. By insulting the sculpture, she had insulted not only Emily's ability to do her job, but the Nos Dada itself, which was on the same level as telling a mother that her fugly kid smells like the permanently damp towel you use to dry down your dog.

Alexis walked to the blurb next to the sculpture before

35

Emily noticed her face. It was predictably long, and full of vague artspeak about immuno-collaborative responses relating to the aesthetic. She double-checked the name at the top. Of all the people, she thought. She should have known.

'This guy,' she said, pointing at the name. 'Hugo Deri Jones. I disturbed him finishing a paste up last night in the Dutch Trader garden. He chucked a bucket of paste over me. I was soaked. It was awful.'

Emily nodded along, almost to herself, and said, 'He's always been like that.'

'I can imagine. He comes across as such an arrogant twat. I couldn't believe what he did. It took me an hour to get it out of my hair.'

'I mean, he's always been a bit of a prankster. He built his brand on interventionism.'

'Covering me in cold paste on a cold night had nothing to do with his "brand".'

Emily stared until Alexis started to feel uncomfortable. Then she said, 'The fact that you don't understand why you should have been grateful for that opportunity is why he is probably going to the Biennale this year and you probably won't ever. You should have documented it and presented it as a collaboration.'

Alexis found herself speechless, but when she tried to laugh at the absurdity of Emily's proposition it came out so fast that it sounded more like a hiss. Emily shrugged and walked towards a few graff tags on a canvas before Alexis could think of a reply.

After five long minutes of standing around watching everyone else in conversation, Alexis walked along the long attic room, turning sideways to make herself as small as possible to pass through the groups, but she didn't see anyone she knew. She went up to a small yellow tent with condom wrappers and beer bottles spilling out at the entrance. She didn't recognise the artist's name, but the blurb said it was called *Millennial Festival Love Story*. What it was in actuality, Alexis thought, was a really bad knockoff of two of Emin's works. But where Emin had made her bed and tent to work cathartically through some of the big events of her life, Alexis couldn't find anything in the essay-disguised-as-a-blurb on the wall to explain what *Millennium Festival Love Story* was trying to say. And the silhouettes on the wall next to it, of men with smartphones chasing after a woman, weren't 'a novel way of approaching the contemporary dating scene', as their own blurb said, but downright problematic.

She looked around the room. They were all the same. Every picture and sculpture, except for hers, was some kind of sight gag. Her own picture had taken near twenty hours to paint and a lifetime of classes, degrees, and pain to get it to look exactly as she wanted. But it now looked out of place, as if she should be embarrassed at the effort it took her to make it.

She wondered why she couldn't find any of her friends. She thought about hanging around the wine table until someone she knew came in when she heard a loud voice from behind her : ay, 'Sure, I love meeting the fans, everything I do is for the f ans.'

And she heard Emily's voice say, 'She's not a "fan", Hugo, she's an artist like you. We were just discussing your work.'

She turned around and saw Emily walking towards her, arm in arm with Hugo. He was wearing a striped T-shirt and the same woolly hat and fingerless gloves of the night before. This time, as he met her eyes, she could tell that he recognised her. He didn't speak, but Alexis looked over at Emily to give her a What The Fuck face and she was already smirking. But before Emily said any more, an artist Alexis vaguely knew approached them – a smart, suited woman with close-cropped silver hair and blunt black glasses. Alexis wondered if she might have just started lecturing. Emily and the artist hugged, then unconsciously, as two old friends sometimes do, they turned slightly away from Alexis and Hugo.

Alexis wanted to leave, but before she had the chance to move, Hugo said, 'Don't expect an apology.'

She felt like slapping him across his face. But instead she said, 'I wasn't going to ask for one.'

Hugo crossed his arms. 'I can't believe you took the piss out of my piece in the pub when you've made this borderline Stuckist monstrosity. It's so earnest, like you actually spent some time on it.'

Alexis looked at Emily, but she was still so deep into her conversation that she didn't hear a thing. She said, 'It's like you said. Not everyone "gets" art.'

Hugo opened his mouth to answer, but before he said anything, Emily turned to face them and said, 'Glad to see you're both getting on. This is my friend Siân, and would you believe it but she's just started working for the Arts Council.'

Hugo shook Siân's hand and talked for half a minute without breathing about how nice it was to meet her. And as Alexis properly introduced herself, all she could think was, so this is Emily's Old White Man.

They exchanged pleasantries as Siân told them what a strong show it was. Then she said, 'So which pieces are yours?'

Hugo said, 'Mine is over by the far wall.'

And Emily said to Siân, 'I wanted to talk to you about that, actually.'

'That was yours?' Siân said. 'It's so crowded down that end I didn't get a chance to stand in front of it for ages. I love it. It's a great piece. Not to denigrate the other artists but I'm so used to going to galleries and seeing the same kind of thing over and over that it's nice to see something new. Can I have a word?'

Alexis watched them walk off down the attic, back towards the sculpture at the far end. She was going to ask him to apply for the Biennale, Alexis was sure of it. Even if he didn't get it he was on their radar now. It was the way the Arts Council worked. Soon he would be a Made Man like the Sicilians.

'I hope you know how humiliating that was for me,' Alexis said, when she remembered she was stood there with Emily.

Emily shrugged and said, 'I'm a bit Darwinian on this kind of thing nowadays. It's not my fault you don't help yourself.'

Alexis shook her head. She turned and walked away.

She had got to the bottom of the stairs when she heard some footsteps behind her. She looked back and saw Siân taking two at a time. 'There appears to be some kind of mistake,' Siân said. 'It isn't that weird sculpture I like. Have you got time for a quick word before you go?'

Alexis said yes, and had to remind herself not to show her enthusiasm on her face. They went back up the stairs and towards the picture. She felt Emily's eyes on her. When they got near, Emily looked away.

'Your picture really stands out here,' Siân said. 'Have you got any hi-res images? We have a few projects coming up soon that you might want to look out for.'

Alexis saw Hugo, down the other end of the hall, disappearing, step by step, as he took the stairs. This was the kind of intervention she liked, Alexis thought, as Siân handed her a business card.

Asking a Shadow to Dance

There was no time to think. The sun was already down, which left Jordan's skin exposed and licked of heat even with his polo shirt buttons done up to the top. He walked back along the street, counting the houses on the way. Down the alley at the back he found the wall to his own garden, dark as the rest under the orange cordial of the Tremorfa sky. Maybe Mum would leave through the front door at the same time and then he wouldn't have to deal with her until the morning.

As soon as he climbed over the wall he knew that it was hopeless. The door to the kitchen was open. All he could see was his mother giving him seagulls from across the garden, one eye on him and one on the rolling boil of her spud-pan.

He saw no point in hanging around. He was feeling pretty hungry anyhow, as he'd just been chilling behind the top shops with some of the boys from the Tremorfire Crew. And smoking a five-fag half-ounce mix didn't half give you the munchies. He walked down the path, ducking under the white flags of his bedding on the line. The kitchen was full of steam, but he couldn't work out if it came from the stove or the top of his mother's head.

His cheeks started to flush from the hot wet room and his mother's cold stare. The only sound in the kitchen came from the four sizzling rashers at the back of the stove, frying with a lisp.

'YOU,' she said, and she pointed her wooden spoon three inches away from his nose. 'Doan think you're havin dinner with us tonight. You were meant to be back hours ago to look after your brother. And I missed the Bingo so your Aunty Joyce will be tampin with you and all.'

He checked his phone for the time and out of habit he almost checked to see if anyone had added to their Insta story, but then he caught his mother stirring the pan into a whirlpool out of the corner of his eye.

'Oh come on,' he said, palms turned up. 'It's gettin light in the nights now and I didn't have no signal.'

He crossed his arms and leaned his hip on the kitchen counter, so she knew that she wasn't going to win. Her brow eased out of its downward point but she was still giving him the side eye.

'And you stinks of smoke again,' she said, throwing too much salt in the pan. 'If your dad was here then he wouldn't have taken this shit from you. So I shouldn't have to either.'

'Well he ain't around,' Jordan said, 'So you can't be pulling that one on me no more.'

And that was all that mattered. There wasn't much else that had mattered recently, ever since one of the younger Silva kids had run up to him in the street last July in front of everyone and told him the bad news from the hospital.

She snapped the wooden spoon down and spread her fingers over the counter as the spud-pan spat on the stove.

'You best watch your chops,' she said, putting the wooden spoon between them. 'And doan you EVER think you can talk to me like that. And I'll say it again. You're lucky that your father ain't here.'

'I couldn't care less,' he said. 'I'm off to my room. And I ain't hungry anyhow.'

His mother chucked the wooden spoon in the sink and marched into the lounge. When she came out she had Tyrone by the wrist and was leading him out through the front door.

41

He knew where she would be going. If his brother was with her then she'd be off to see Aunty Joyce up the road. So he turned the hobs off to wait for her as he ate the rashers out the pan.

He thought about what she would say. They called her Juicy Joyce up the New Dock Tavern cos everyone wanted a squeeze. But all the old boys who gave her the eye didn't know what Jordan knew, being family and all that. If you squeezed her the wrong way she'd be far more sour than even the sharpest lemon. It was probably why the only man who could ever handle her was Big Steve Silva, as no one wanted to mess with him, not even her.

But on seeing his aunty slam the front door a few minutes later looking like she wanted to chew his face, all Jordan could think of was how he should have taken Joey Silva up on his offer when he nicked his brother's knuckle dusters and wanted to swap them for a teenth of sticky black.

Every time Joyce took a step nearer he could see the white skin in the folds of her arms and neck where the sunbeds couldn't reach. There was no cheeky smile and no asking after Stacey when she got close. Instead she got right in his face so he could smell the peroxide in her hair and count her overlapping teeth. She told him how he's an arsehole and he's let his mother down and if he's not careful he'll end up just like his father and look where that got him, bent round the steering wheel of some random car that wasn't even his after he got blue-lighted.

Jordan let her get in his face, because it didn't matter what she said. Joyce wasn't his mother's blood so it was nothing to do with her. They were only related through his father and he wasn't around any more anyway. And as she was with a Silva now she had taken sides even before the accident.

He folded his arms and looked at her down the straight

edge of his nose. He knew exactly the right words to use in his own house because he'd heard his father say the same thing.

He said, 'Don't treat me like I'm some kind of a cunt.'

At first, he could tell that Joyce didn't know what to do. As she looked back at him, Jordan noticed that she had shrunk, almost as if she was being crushed inwards.

'I'll pretend I didn't hear that,' she said, almost in a whisper.

'I said, Aunty Joyce, don't treat me like I'm some kind of a cunt.'

Her mouth was slightly open and she might have been shaking her head, or it might have been her whole body.

'That's it,' she said. 'If you won't listen to me and you won't listen to your mother, we'll just have to see if you will listen to Big Steve.'

As Joyce walked back down the hall and let herself out, it felt like someone had slammed a syringe full of adrenalin down his throat. One of the reasons you knew Big Steve Silva meant business was because his nose wasn't like an overripe, squashed banana. It's like dad always used to say. It's not the ones who look like they've had a few hidings you should be worried about. Big Steve made people listen. Once, he made the whole street give blood when the van was outside Tyrone's Primary just by going round every house and having a quiet word. All because one of the old boys he knew from down the Ninian stand on a Saturday afternoon had told him about his daughter in the hospice. No one messed with Big Steve.

There was only one thing to do. He had to talk with his mother before Big Steve got to her first. He'd already seen some of the older boys like Matthew Postgate get a slap just for giving chops when Big Steve had a smoke outside the

New Dock Tavern. And it was skittles night on a Tuesday so he wouldn't be in anyway. So Jordan left his house and walked down the yellow, white and pinks of the terrace. They glowed under the lampshade clouds above and it felt like they were all watching him. He opened the door to Aunty Joyce's house, no point knocking, and walked straight down the hall, past the stairs, and into the kitchen. But there was no one there. Then he checked the lounge, and the news was on but nobody was watching it. So he went back in the kitchen and sat down at the table to wait for his mum or Aunty Joyce to show up, while he leaned back in his chair and tried to slow his breathing.

When the front door clicked, Jordan looked up and caught Big Steve Silva's eyes looking back at him, olive as his skin, from under his neanderbrow. He was carrying a blue plastic bag in his left hand and a smoke in the other.

Their eyes stayed locked until Big Steve was sat down at the table. Jordan being unable to break the gaze and Big Steve unwilling.

From the bag, Big Steve pulled out a can of beer and opened it. They watched it mutter. Ten seconds went past. 'It's best to pour your beer,' Big Steve said, 'after it's stopped all the spittin. That way, it ain't gonna froth up the glass and spill all over your hand.'

They listened to the fizzing from the can die down before anything else was said. Big Steve got two glasses out of the cupboard and put them on the table. Jordan caught his eyes again, but he didn't say anything.

'You best fill your glass quick,' Big Steve said.

Jordan didn't move at first, caught out between the stern look on Big Steve's face and his gesturing hand, big as a tugboat's rudder. Then Big Steve slid the can over and Jordan poured the beer in one long pull.

He choked on his first sip, and he remembered what his dad said once. Big Steve liked to drink the type of beer where if you added a splash of red diesel then you could probably run a van off the stuff. The sip felt like his first and last.

Big Steve leaned forward on the table. His forearm looked as thick as Jordan's calf, with twice the tan at that. 'It ain't right to give your mother chops,' he said.

It wasn't quite a threat but it was still enough to make Jordan go cold. But he'd seen enough in the way of handbags to know what to do. Someone was always on the doorstep saying something like that to his father. And Big Steve had no right to lecture him anyway. He hadn't even been in the family long enough to be called Uncle Steve. As far as Jordan was concerned, he was still a Silva.

Jordan put both his hands on the table, palms turned down, and straightened his back. 'You best stay out of my family's fuckin business,' he shouted. 'All you fuckin Silvas are the fuckin same, that's what my dad said. Just cos you can fuck everyone up you thinks everyone has to do what you says. Well I doesn't have to do any fuckin thing you tells me.'

But Big Steve just took another can out of the bag and cracked it open. Jordan knew then that he'd sounded like the Suldanas' Jack Russell from across the road.

'You about finished?' Big Steve said. 'You got all those horrible words out your system? Good. Cos now you can talk like a man.'

He had never felt so small. And next to Big Steve, with his chin that you could crack nuts on, it felt even worse. Jordan took his hands off the table and put them under his knees, so Big Steve couldn't see them tremble.

Big Steve tried again. 'Now if you thinks I'm gonna listen to a scrote like you call me every name under the sun in my own yard then you best get your swede checked,' he said.

'Cos not only have you upset your mother and your Aunty Joyce but now you upset me and all. And now you'll be lucky to leave this house the same scrote as you were when you came in.'

Big Steve grabbed Jordan by the crown with one hand and made him stand up. He led him out the room and down the hall. Jordan could tell that Big Steve could tighten his grip like a vice if he wanted and leave him with a skull looking like he was pulled out with forceps at birth, but instead it felt like Big Steve was handling him as a Staffie bitch would when carrying her pups by the scruff.

At the foot of the stairs, Big Steve let go. He put a finger to his lips, and urged Jordan up with his paddle of a hand. On the landing they stopped outside the first bedroom. There was just about enough space. The door was closed but not in its catch, but they didn't go in. Big Steve opened the door just enough to let the light through the crack. He grabbed Jordan by the top of his skull again. He placed his head at the join, just below the second hinge, so he could see right into the room.

It took a second to take everything in.

His mother sat on the bed to the left of Aunty Joyce. She was staring at the rug over the floorboards. She was holding a tissue and she was looking down with eyes of gentle red.

She dabbed at the leakage. Jordan realised he had never seen his mother that way before. For the first time, he wasn't seeing her as the cow who came out into the street to call him in for dinner or as the sad act who got dressed up for the Bingo every Tuesday. Because for the first time in his life, Jordan had seen the same person that everybody else saw. He was seeing the woman who was bringing up two young sons on her own, the woman who still grieved for her lost lover, the woman who hardly ever went down the New Dock

Tavern like all her friends but took as her weekly respite a single night of Bingo. And he knew for once that it was him who was making her look like this.

He watched them for half a minute, and then Big Steve grabbed his ear and pulled him away from the door. They snuck back into the kitchen.

'Tell me what you saw,' Big Steve said.

Jordan looked at his glass on the table. He said, 'I never seen my mother cry before. Not even at the funeral.'

Big Steve stretched back and exhaled. 'That's because she was staying strong for you and Tyrone,' he said. 'But every week since last summer your Mother Sal comes here and has a chat with your Aunty Joyce before the Bingo. And all she ever does is ask where did she go wrong.'

Big Steve undid the buckle on his belt, slid it from its loops with one hand, and placed it on the table.

'I never meant to make her feel like that,' Jordan said, and he wiped his nose and blinked.

Big Steve stood up again. 'Let me tell you what I knows about life,' he said, making the belt taut at arm's length. 'There comes a time when you're given a choice. Sooner or later you has to become the person you're gonna be for the rest of the time you got left. But sometimes it takes a bit of nudgin to get there.'

Jordan got up. 'Please don't hurt me,' he said, with his hands out in front. 'I knows I done wrong, Big Steve, I knows I done wrong.'

Big Steve said, 'I'm gonna do somethin much worse than hit you. Now finish your beer so you can go say sorry to your mother.'

Big Steve flexed the belt once more, and between Jordan's sips of beer he snapped the leather on the table. The house trembled like the midnight train was going past and Jordan's ears stung, but all he could think was how drinking a strong beer wasn't much of a punishment.

After a dozen or so smacks of the table Big Steve stopped and gestured for Jordan to follow him. They went up the stairs and Big Steve let Jordan go into the room. His mother stood up. Before he'd even said anything he had added fifteen years to her face. She bunched her eyes and tried not to cry. He went to her and hugged her and never wanted to let her go.

'Oh my boy, my beautiful, beautiful boy,' she said. 'I'm so sorry. I'm so, so sorry. I didn't know what else to do or where else to go.'

Her forehead started to wrinkle upwards as she looked into his eyes for forgiveness. She even managed a small smile. And it was at that moment he knew what Big Steve had done, as he understood what it was to make his mother cry. Because behind her weak smile was everything he had never understood before.

Things That Make
the Heart Beat Faster

RHYS

While we wait for the pills we bought off the old wreckhead to smash in, Rhiannon and I climb a tree near the sound system to build a spliff. This way, the crusties and pikeys who never share can't ask for thirds. I hold the three-deck of Rizla while cupping my hands, so Rhi can crumble in the tobacco and lemon haze mix with all her fingers.

From our vantage point halfway up the tree, I can see right over to the other side of the entrance to Castle Cavern. All the spotlights and car headlights point towards the DJ on the crooked scaffold rig, about twenty metres from our tree. The older heads say the best illumination is when a police helicopter flies overhead, shining its light onto the dance pit at the entrance to the cave itself.

I look down at the crowd while Rhi rips off some card from the edge of the Rizla packet and rolls a roach. Next to a Clio near the dance pit is a girl with long brown dreadlocks about the same age as us. She's flapping her arms and stamping her feet into the ground. She scrapes her fingers through her dreads and screams. 'Fuckin hell, I remember her,' Rhiannon says. 'She was in the year above, I swear. She's called Elin or something.'

I strain my eyes but I can't quite make her out, and I wonder if the pills are kicking in. I say, 'Never seen her before.'

'She didn't have the dreads in school, but they don't care about that kinda thing when you're in college.'

The girl starts shouting, so I turn my head so I can better hear what she's saying.

'I'm melting,' she says. 'I'm melting, I'm dying, oh help me please, oh help me.'

A man puts his arm around her, but she shrugs him off. I could recognise that headband over the shot of curly hair anywhere, as I've been looking at it most of my life; it's our cousin Warren, who we had got a lift to the party with. The girl starts to run, trips, and hits her head on the ground, then she ricochets off the floor and ends up on her hands and knees. She grabs handfuls of air and presses them against her stomach. She grabs more handfuls and shoves them into her mouth, but she can't keep up with herself and ends up curled in like a foetus. We can see the sweat in her dreads and across her face from where we are up the tree. She coughs and something yellow slides down her cheek. I look at Rhiannon. She's stopped making the spliff to watch her, too.

'That's spooked me out a bit. What do you think she's taken?' I say, chewing a spare Rizla.

'No clue,' she answers. 'Nothing that I ever wanna try.'

Rhiannon wraps the spliff into a long cone, puts a flame to the larger twisted end, and inhales. I see Warren walking by towards the four-quarter snare of techno from the rig. I shout his name, and he climbs the ten feet up the tree to join us. He must have taken something good cos he practically runs up it and is plonking himself down for afters in what feels like less than a second. 'What was up with that girl? Off it, she was,' I say.

'I know, cuz. Can't handle her drugs, that one. Thinks she's Pac-Man, the way she munches her pills.'

Rhiannon passes the spliff to Warren. 'What pills did she take? We just dropped some, see.'

'She took a 2C-I. Bangers, they are. I had some the other day, it's like taking acid and ecstasy at the same time. You get the oneness without the paranoia, and some pretty fractals whenever you look at lights. Gets you mashed for hours.'

'We dropped some tonight. We got them off some old guy,' I say, as Rhiannon passes me the spliff.

Warren looks at me but doesn't speak, then slaps his forehead and lets his hand slide down the flat bridge of his nose.

'You know, when you get a pill, you can't know how strong they are unless you know who's made them. It all depends on how fucked the crusty was when the pills were pressed, especially if they picked them up from someone else. Could have come from the 'Dam or London. That's why they've all got a little logo. Generally speaking, if they've got cars, it means you'll rush fast: they're cut with a bit of speed. If it's a peace sign, they've added a bit of ketamine: you'll be chilled out. Who'd you buy them off?'

'His name was Davy John. These ones were white,' I say.

'Mine were white, too,' says Rhiannon. 'But I noticed on the front that there was a big letter P. I didn't see Rhys's.'

I take a toke of the spliff as Warren looks at us with half a smile on his face.

'Davy John's a bloody nutcase,' he says. 'He's so destructive with his drugs. The council should employ him as a Drugs Disposal Unit.'

He passes me the spliff and I take a long suck. 'That crusty who was trying to swallow her own imaginary intestines. She had one of Davy's pills.'

Rhiannon looks at me, then at Warren. 'I double-dropped,' she says.

'Me too,' I say. 'Davy said we'd need two each.'

Warren booms out a laugh, and when he's done he says,

51

'Sign of a good businessman, that is. When did you take them?'

'Dunno, say, midnight, about ten minutes ago.'

'Well, it's too late now. Even if you stick your fingers down your throat, you'll still have the stuff in your bloodstream, cos that's what psychedelics are like. See that crusty?'

He points at the girl we used to know from school. I look over, and she's licking the ground.

'Yes,' I say.

'You got fifty minutes, cuz. At 1am, you'll both be like her.'

WARREN

I regrets saying it as soon as the words trip over my tongue, cos the last thing you needs when you've just dropped is a reason to fall into paranoia. Lucky I caught them when they were still in the waiting room. There I am, trying to be the good big cousin by taking them to a party and instead I'm gonna be acting the shepherd all night.

It's always best for first-timers if there's a straight-head present. I'd only taken a little speed, maybe only half a gram in a small bottle of Smirnoff. I decides to look after them myself. Dad would drown me if he found out I killed his only niece and nephew.

After finishing the spliff, we goes down the branches. They both fly down the tree, one in front of the other with hoods up, each hanging off a branch and walking down with their hands, just like they would when I used to take them down Roath Park as nippers. I guessed it wouldn't be long before they were both rolling around with the dreadlocked girl.

'Guys,' I say, when I gets to the bottom. 'I'm gonna stay with you to make sure you're all right. I won't let you end up like the crusty girl.'

Rhiannon's pupils are already starting to dilate. The black centres are overtaking the grey of her irises, looming over them like the dark canopy of the forest.

Just the one rig is needed in the Castle Cavern, as the echo bounces around the canyon towards the Garth Mountains – anyone the other side towards Tongwynlais is unaware that 25k of sound is beating a ton-two-five decibel of techno into the ears of two thousand revellers. We skirts slowly around the outskirts of the dance pit, watching the pikeys and mash-heads raving away, hitting each other, slamming the speakers with their hands and shaking the DJ's scaffold stage. But after two songs, I notices both of them staring into space. Rhiannon has already started to feast on her own gums like some kind of toothless old crone chewing a banana, clenching her jaw and grinding her teeth. They didn't have long.

I takes them away from the music, to the other side of the tree where I met them.

'Guys, skin up,' I say. Anything to keep them occupied.

Tougher than I thought, this was going to be. I takes the tobacco off Rhiannon and makes myself a roll-up.

My third drag, and she still hasn't stuck two Rizlas together. Every time she holds them, she stares or starts to giggle. Rhys is sat on the floor, trying to mix the tobacco through the herb, but even with his palm near the level of his head, he can't see what he's doing. He starts to rock.

I don't even need my own drugs no more. Not when I've got these two sorry cases to look after. It's like when all the family would get together for a birthday or a funeral and all the adults would get pissed and tell each other stories and I'd be left with these two making sure they didn't go under the kitchen sink and convince each other the Persil non-bio was actually sherbet. 'Stay by here, guys. I'm off to get a draw,' I say. 'And no matter what you do, don't leave this spot. Don't move. I'll be back in three.'

I skims the oscillation of ravers to the far corner, out of the echo of the bass and drum, and finds Davy John with the girl from earlier. He's too busy dowsing her with a bottle of water to notice me.

Not hard to swap some Class A's for a bit of smoke, and I'm back after swapping my pills for an eighth of sticky with a pikey from Nantyglo.

But by the time I comes back, they've gone.

RHIANNON

There's nothing better than taking drugs till your brain vibrates. Another wave of the pills kicks in, so I join the gyrating, rocking crowd. It doesn't feel like I do this to dance, but to be thrown about by the bass. I get in and am dancing like no one's watching, marching on the spot. Swinging my head from side to side like I don't care. The bassline is going at about 175 bpm, which is about the same as what my ticker is doing.

I look about. Everyone's wearing a random combination of tight trousers, thick-rimmed glasses with empty frames, Grandad suspenders, fedoras, complicated haircuts, or check shirts with all the buttons done up. A few even have aviators, even though the lighting from the rig only comes on every other song. Then, on the edge of the pit I see Davy John. He's holding two pots and has had his whole bald head painted. One side red, the other side yellow.

'Mate, fucking blowers, those 2C-Is,' I say to him when I walk over. 'I've started coming up already and I only dropped half-hour ago.'

He smiles and shows me his missing teeth. Warren told me

about this once: excessive speed consumption. It takes calcium to process the phet, and if you take too much, your body takes some from its store of teeth and bones.

'Glad you like 'em,' he says, as he looks down at my boots. 'I press these ones myself. You okay?'

I look down at my own feet and they're stomping away without me. 'Yeah man, I'm just dying to dance. I need to move,' I say.

'Looks like you already started, gul. Go enjoy yourself. Just make sure you look the part.' He dips his hands into the yellow pot and starts to smear them all over my face. I come up hard again and the pills make me feel the calico of his hands, rough as a length of old rope, through the butter-like texture of the paint. He pulls down my hood and puts his hands in the red pot, Then he runs his hands through my hair and brings it all down past my neck. 'There you are, see. Now you look the part.' He gives me a wink. 'You want more pills?'

After dropping another small one for luck, I join the crowd in the middle of the pit, and start punching the subwoofers to the backbeat, jumping up and down, putting one hand in the air when I recognise a tune. Never enjoyed techno before this, but every repetition makes sense, and I can see how the DJ's mind works. I give him a nod, and his baseball cap nods back.

Eventually, I notice that the bank holiday humidity is catching up with my lungs, and before too long I'm struggling to breathe, the heat of the low clouds drawing all the moisture from my mouth. I catch eyes with this crusty in camo trousers who has earrings going all the way up his lobe. He leans over and tries to say something, but I can't hear him. I hold my hands out and carry on dancing. He puts his fingertip on the first small pointy bit of cartilage at the front of my ear. 'THIS BASS IS SO BAD,' he shouts, and I'm so surprised I can hear him that my heart tries to combust, 'THAT IT COULD RIP YOUR CLOTHES OFF.' He looks around. 'PEOPLE KNOWS YOU AIN'T GOT INTIMATE PIERCINGS COS YOU WOULDA CLIMAXED BY NOW.'

'Fucking hell, mate,' I shout to him. 'You're old enough to be my dad.'

I decide I need a drink and a sit down. I leave him to dance and I spot a chair at the edge of the dance pit. I walk up and throw my hoodie over it, and sit down as a wave takes over, and all I can do is sit and stare and take it. But the chair starts to move, and then I realise that nobody brings chairs to raves. I'm sitting on some crusty or pikey or Valley commando, sat on the floor with his legs tucked into his chin, trying to rediscover reality like I am. I jump up, picking my hoodie up off his head.

'Sorry, mate. I thought you was a chair,' I say.

I disappear off into the crowd, before he catches my face under my mask of paint and chemical bravado.

RHYS

I stop trying to skin up as soon as Rhiannon leaves. Hits me it does, like a thud on the back of the head, and I feel like I want to curl up and go to sleep. It isn't that I didn't want the spliff, it's just that I don't care any more whether it gets rolled or not. All I want to do is stare at the dancers and let my head fill with its own sense of emptiness, and let my mind meld to the timbre of the synth.

It could have been hours that I've been here, but the same tune is still playing. I don't care, as long as I can relax. I feel the need to have a piss, so I push myself up off the base of the tree. I walk around it and go into this small copse of trees, which are swaying from side to side in the breeze.

Halfway through my piss I hear someone shout, and then another shout from behind me. The trees part away, and I realise that I'm at the entrance to a cave in a forest and there's no breeze for miles, and I'm standing in a group of crusties, with my dick in my hand, pissing on someone's steel toe caps. I dribble all over my jeans as I run away, to the other side of the cavern, and I really feel the need to sit back down.

I stare at the dancers again. I don't know how long. The music muffles, and everything goes black. I feel a bump on my head and I still don't care. I stay like this for what could be an hour, or maybe twenty seconds.

Soon as it's black, it's all light again, and I'm staring up at the never-ending industrial sunset. A patch of colour catches my eye, and I look to my right. In the dim light, I can see a flower. A tall, gangly pansy, with eyes wide as car headlights staring back at me. I didn't know what to say, but the pansy answers for me. 'Sorry mate. I thought you was a chair.'

The pansy snakes off into the crowd.

I decide right there that I'm never taking anything harder than a cup of coffee again.

DAVY JOHN

There's something in us all that makes us wanna get smashed. It's always been there in everyone. Back in the day, people used to shant beer instead of water. Their smokes were ten times stronger, so you would get a headrush just from looking at a pipe. You would smash as much opium as you could to cure everything from a cough to a hangover to a sawn-off leg. And fuck the afternoon pick-me-up cuppa when you could have a mug of brandy and half a teaspoon of cocaine instead.

Even nowadays, at any one time half the world's tribes are fucked on some mad colourful frog. Getting off it on drugs is a part of you, and you're letting yourself down if you deny it to yourself.

Past the worse of it she was, by the time they changed from techno to drum'n'bass. We're sat facing each other, me and this dreadlocked girl I sold some pills to earlier. I could pretend that she begged me for them, but really I just wanted the sell. And now it was my turn to look after her until she could look after herself.

She was starting to understand what I said again. After her third bottle of water I decide enough is enough, so she doesn't drown in her body. I stand up and pat my pockets to look for the bar of chocolate I've got somewhere. It's the oldest trick, the insulin spike. But just as I find it in the breast of my jacket, the red smoking one I got at Oxfam, I see Warren walking up to me, pace like rolling thunder. No smile from my old spar, so I wonder how much and of what he's been taking.

'Yes, Warren. Long time, long time,' I say. 'Good turnout tonight, must be about two thousand people down.'

He gives me no answer until he's three inches from my face. 'Don't give me that shit, bruv. I'd make you bite the kerb, if you didn't take so much speed,' he says, like he's spitting a round of uzi bullets.

'What you chattin?' I say. I take a half-step back. You never know what someone else has been taking in a place like this.

'What the fuck are you up to, bruv. Selling pills to kids. Look at her.' He points at the girl with the dreads. 'And my cousins. They've only just done their GCSEs, for fuck's sake.'

'Spar, I don't know what you're talking. What little bird been saying what?'

'Those kids you sold the 2C-Is to. What are you up to, man? You trying to kill them?'

A dangerous game this is, but I smile. For all of how people spends loadsa money on drugs, there's still loads more mad drugs inside you than you could ever steal and munch from a chemist. All the contraband does is heighten your natural state. And instead of the natural state lasting a few seconds, it goes on for hours. I can't help it, and I break out into a low chuckle. I put my hands out in front, like I'm warming them on the fire of Warren's temper, letting him know that he'll get his answer when I'm ready. 'I'm not that irresponsible, spar. I sold them duds.'

He throws his hands in the air. 'So you knocked my cousins. Well that's just fuckin great.'

I sit on the floor next to the girl, and take out my tobacco pouch. Warren looks down at me on the floor but he stays stood up. I pat the ground until he squats.

'Trust me, spar,' I say. 'They won't know. As long as they think that they've taken something, their serotonin will be up, and their imaginations will do the rest. They'll have the best time of their lives, and they won't even wake up tomorrow with a comedown. I done them a favour. They can tell all their spars what a great time they had without having done any harm.'

He takes my pouch and starts to roll himself a cigarette, and smokes it without a filter. He gives it to the dreadlock girl and she starts to do the same. 'Glad to see you're back with us,' I say to her. 'What do you think?'

'I think no one should ever feel like I felt earlier,' she says, as she puts some tobacco in a Rizla.

I offer my lighter to Warren. 'See? Those two kept badgering me and in the end, I gave in. I gave one of them caffeine pills and the other one valium. They were barely on the dizzy side of sober. Their minds did the rest. This just gives them bragging rights to say they tried it.'

Warren gives me back my pouch and leans back, spreading his legs on the floor.

'You swears down?' he says.

'They'll never do them again. They're stoners, not ravers. They only took them to look hard in front of each other. I know it, you know it. Weren't we the same?' I stub my filter on the ground, and flick it into the darkness. 'They got Pro-Plus and diazepam. Caffeine pills and what was left of my 'script.' I look at the girl. 'I know now not to sell the hard stuff to those who aren't ready.'

I take the chocolate out of my pocket and give it to her.

ELIN

After a few minutes of looking, we find him on the periphery of the dancing area, with his knees brought up to his chin. 'Must have got the tamazes, that one,' my new friend Warren whispers over the clattering music. I walk up to him. He's about my age, and I swear I know him from somewhere. Warren stays a few feet back, behind us.

'This patch taken?' I say, and point at the ground. No answer. 'How are you doing tonight, having a good time?'

He brings his legs down from his chin and crosses them, but keeps his shoulders by his ears. 'I've made an absolute arse of myself, the past few hours,' he says. 'I pissed all over some guy's shoe and had a flower tell me I'm a chair. I'm buzzing hard.'

'I dropped tonight, too. I took a few 2C-Is. What did you take?'

'That's what I took, and all. I think I saw you earlier after you dropped, you scared me.' He picks up a stick.

I choose to ignore his comment, and continue with what I was planning on saying. 'You got them off Davy John, too?'

'Yeah man,' he says. 'Blowers, they are. Not sure if I can handle this.'

I put my hand on his knee. He looks at my face. 'It's Rhys, isn't it? You're OK, you are. Davy John gave you valium instead of a 2C-I. Probably why you feel so stoned. That's how you're feeling, isn't it?'

He looks down, envelopes his hand on my wrist and places it back on my lap. 'What the hell did he do that for? Fucking crusty. They're all the fuckin same, the lot of them. Knocking us just because we didn't grow up in a caravan. Who the hell does he think he is?'

He throws the stick on the ground. He looks up a bit, across the horizon of weaving heads that make up the dance pit at the foot of the cavern. Before I can answer, he stands up and gets on his toes and he starts to smile. I stand up to see what he's looking at.

'I can see my sister over there. She's dancing like my dad at our brother's wedding, but she looks just like a pansy in my mam's back garden.'

'Look at her,' I say. 'She's having the time of her life, isn't she? And she didn't even need to take anything hardcore. She just had something like you had.'

'I saw her earlier,' he says, as he shakes his head. 'I thought she was a flower.' He turns his head to look at me and smiles.

'You're not going to tell her, are you?' I say.

He relaxes his shoulders. 'Only if you don't tell her I thought she was a flower.'

We both look over at Rhiannon, and the rest of the dancers in the floor of the clearing. It would be hours before the sun came up, and maybe a day or two before the more hardcore people like Davy John started to leave. I offer him some of my water and he drinks it. Soon we would be able to see the dancers properly, the girls with one side of their heads shaved and the skinny boys with their bumbags slung across a shoulder. We sit there, waiting for the sky to go full deep blue before it turns light to signal the new day. But until that happened, we would keep on passing the bottle between us, taking little sips, enjoying the riffs and the synths and the bass for what they are.

One of the Cullens

He was already ten minutes late for meeting Mim, so Glenn bunny-hopped onto the pavement and sped towards the side street. He got to the corner and almost bowled into some guy coming the other way, and Glenn had to swerve back on the road so they didn't crash.

It was no surprise he almost hit into him. The guy was solid. They were maybe the same height but the guy's neck looked as thick as one of Glenn's legs.

'GET ON THE FUCKIN ROAD,' the guy shouted, as Glenn turned up the side street the guy had just walked down. Glenn looked back from his bike and said, 'Oh, do fuck off.'

The man turned and Glenn had never seen someone look so offended before. It was as if everything bad that had ever happened was all because of Glenn.

The man said, 'GET OFF YA FUCKIN BIKE AND SAY THAT.'

But Glenn kept cycling slowly while looking backwards and giving the man some Vs.

The man started to walk and he broke out into a jog and Glenn said, 'Come on, no neck, you could do with a jog,' and the man stopped.

Glenn turned round and went to keep on cycling but he heard the man shout, 'YOU FUCKIN WANKER, GET OFF THE FUCKIN BIKE, IF I EVER SEES YOU AGAIN I'M GONNA SMASH YOU. I'LL FUCKIN SMASH YOU.'

And Glenn just cycled down the side street towards the

alley at the other end and onwards to Mim's house. It was no biggie, upsetting a rando, even if he did feel a bit guilty.

* * *

Mim still didn't have the money but he swore down he'd get it sorted. They left the bike at Mim's and walked through town to the Jobcentre, and Glenn got to hear the opening lines his chugger work colleagues used when they didn't recognise him without his Save the Turtles coat. They walked into the Jobcentre, and Glenn nodded at the security guard as Mim took a ticket.

Glenn said, 'I don't miss this place.'

Mim said, 'Can't blame you.'

Mim's ticket said 255 and they'd just called out 241. They got their phones out and started scrolling.

After showing Mim how many hits his latest video had got they heard some shouting coming from one of the booths. They heard a man shout, 'A CHEQUE WON'T FUCKIN DO, I NEEDS MY FUCKIN BRASS TODAY.'

They looked over. The man was standing. He had a shaved head and a neck like a concrete bollard. It was the guy Glenn had almost run into.

'He's never gonna get anywhere,' Mim said. 'When they fuck up you never make demands, you have to tell them you got no money in the world and you're gonna die. Anything but shout at them.'

Glenn put his hood up.

The security guard went up to the man. He mumbled something and the man turned around and pointed and said, 'YOU BEST BACK THE FUCK AWAY OR IMMA FUCKIN SMASH YOU.' The security guard held his hands up and walked back. Mim said, 'Oh shit, it's one of the Cullens.'

The man turned to the desk and snatched the cheque and walked towards them.

Glenn sank down into his seat, but the Cullen walked past without looking at them and went out the door, and everyone started talking again.

Mim said, 'You look like my mum last Christmas when she had gastroenteritis. Go the Spoons round the corner, the toilets here are grim.'

Glenn pulled his hood down and said, 'That's that guy I told to fuck off.'

Mim laughed then choked and started to cough. Glenn got up and filled a cup with water from the cooler. He walked back and held it out as Mim whispered, 'I can't believe you flipped off one of the Cullens.'

'Which Cullen is that one?'

Mim took a sip of water. 'I'm not sure,' he said. 'He's either the one who went down for breaking into a salvage yard and smashing the guard dog with a hammer or he's the one who drove around for four days with that nonce in his boot. They all kinda look the same with that big neck.'

They called 255, and Glenn was left on his own feeling very, very cold.

* * *

Two days later and Glenn was just about hitting target. He needed one sign-up an hour to make bonus, but having Save the Turtles on the back of your coat didn't have quite the same effect on the public as Save the Children did.

He hadn't been able to stop anyone for twenty-five minutes, and he was starting to feel depressed. He was trying to get eye contact with anyone he could, and not just those people he felt like he was an expert at getting to sign, which was basically just blokes exactly like him of about the same age.

He looked up the street past the mums and kids. And then he saw him.

The Cullen was walking towards him, walking like he had stones in both boots, romping and stomping as if he was trying to cover as much ground as possible in a single step.

Glenn turned round. If he could just talk to someone then maybe he could pretend that the Cullen wasn't there. Maybe the Cullen wouldn't notice him or the Cullen wouldn't want to start beef if he had an ally.

He saw a woman with straight black hair and big hoops, and he said, 'I love those earrings, you have to tell me where you got them so I can get them for my sister's birthday.'

'That's what you said to me last week,' she said, and while he thought of something, anything to say, she laughed and said, 'I was in Tenerife last week, I just wanted to see what face you'd make.'

He asked her about her holiday, and about the earrings and she told him she got them from Claire's Accessories and he thanked her, and the Cullen still hadn't walked past so he slid into his turtle spiel as if it was the most natural thing in the world. She kept looking over her shoulder as if she had somewhere to be, but she listened to every word he said and he was going wildly off script and talking about his videos even. And he realised that they had something of a rapport, and he couldn't remember if the Cullen had even walked past or not cos he was too busy getting lost somewhere in her eyes.

He remembered about his target and went back to script. He said, 'Does supporting our work saving the turtles sound like something that would interest you?'

'I'm gonna have to say no,' she said.

He looked behind him. The Cullen was gone. The rest of

his team were all in conversations and Bryce the new team leader was nowhere.

He said, 'Does going for a drink sound like something that would interest you instead?'

She smiled and picked up his lanyard with his name on it and said, 'I'll find you on Facebook.'

He watched her walk away into the crowd. Three minutes later, he got a friend request through from Hannah Tremayne.

That afternoon, he had the most sign-ups on the team.

* * *

They met late on the Saturday afternoon for a coffee, but they soon shared a bottle of red over some tapas, and they didn't stop talking once. Hannah lived by herself and she wasn't scared to tell him that she had not long come out of a long relationship (and after the second glass that Glenn shouldn't worry, she split up with him) and Glenn thought that the way this was going, he would be seeing this flat she lived in pretty damn soon.

They left the tapas place and they were feeling merry but they were still too full for dancing. Glenn took her to the Spoons next door because it was the closest place, and they could get a booth to themselves. The bar was three deep. Glenn was just looking at the gin on the shelf when Hannah said, 'I'll go save us a booth,' and she walked away without waiting to hear his answer.

Funny how she walked away like that, he thought. But fair enough.

He got near the front and somehow elbowed his way to the bar. He ordered two Singapore Slings and as the bartender turned to make them he heard someone down the line say, 'NO, I GAVE YOU A FUCKIN TWENTY.'

He looked over. There, speaking to one of the managers in a black shirt, was the Cullen.

He turned his face to the right and looked down. He told the bartender to keep the change.

He went back to the booth the long way round so he wouldn't have to walk past the Cullen. He was still arguing with the manager when he left.

They were practically necking their drinks as they talked, and he felt her knee touch his and she didn't move it away. Glenn forgot all about the Cullen. But then they heard a solid slap and a few people at the bar started shouting and Glenn looked over.

The manager was being dragged over the bar while a bouncer was trying to get two Cullens off him. The other one was definitely a Cullen because he had the neck like a demijohn. The Cullen Glenn knew turned to look at the bouncer and elbowed him once and the bouncer dropped to the floor. He turned back and grabbed the manager with both hands and the two Cullens dropped him on their side of the bar.

Glenn heard him say, 'I TOLD YOU IT WAS A FUCKIN TWENTY BUT YOU HAD TO GET ALL FUCKIN SMART.'

Glenn wanted to leave, but he didn't know if he had any power in his legs.

'I can't be arsed with this,' Hannah said. 'I've had enough of town. Come back to mine and have a coffee.'

Glenn felt his back straighten. They grabbed their coats and walked towards the door. The other two bouncers had joined in. The Cullen Glenn didn't know was wrestling on the floor with another guy in a dark blue shirt and the Cullen he did know was punching two of the bouncers. Hannah walked slow and kept turning back to see.

'You know who that is, don't you?' Glenn said.

Hannah stopped walking. She turned to look one last time, then looked at Glenn like she was trying to see what was behind his face.

'He's one of the Cullens,' she said.

* * *

Their taxi pulled up on a Victorian terrace full of brightly coloured doors overlooking some school playing fields. Glenn got his tenner in the driver's hand first. Hannah let him in then closed the front door quietly, and whispered that she didn't want to wake the old grump on the first floor, and they walked through to the kitchen at the back.

She put a slug of whisky and a teaspoon each of sugar and instant coffee in a mug as the kettle boiled. They sat down at the kitchen table.

'So you can't just want to be a chugger,' she said. 'Tell me what you would do if you owned your own house and all your bills were paid for.'

He started to tell her about his videos, and how if he had the money and the studio he would create Gilliamesque stop-motion animations that took ten hours to create one minute of film but he wouldn't care, it would be all he would do, and she didn't take her eyes off him and he realised that she had somehow moved closer and there was something of a knowing smile on her face, and she sipped her coffee and she was closer still, and he was still going on about his hopes and dreams and he could practically feel her breath on his cheeks she was so close, and he realised that he could probably be saying anything right now and neither of them would remember or care, because the important thing was that he was saying it to her.

And he had just run out of steam and they were so close and he leaned in but he heard a bang and a bang and she

69

turned her head, and they heard a bang and a bang again, and she got out of her chair and walked out the kitchen.

And it was all going so well.

He walked into the front room. She hadn't turned the light on. He heard three quick bangs. She was at the curtains, moving one just enough to the side to see what was going on. She flicked it back into place and took a step back.

He could see how heavy she was breathing. She looked up and saw him, and the way she looked at him wide and bright made him realise that, for a second, she thought he was someone else.

She walked over and put her mouth to his ear.

'It's my ex,' she said. 'He hasn't been taking the split very well.'

A bang came from the window and she shuddered. It sounded like the pane was about to fall through. Glenn heard a voice say, 'I KNOWS YOU'RE IN THERE, HAN. I JUST WANTS TO TALK.'

He knew that voice.

It couldn't be.

He went to the curtain as she did. He moved it enough to see outside with one eye.

It was the Cullen. Glenn saw him bang the front door. He was holding one of his arms across his chest.

Glenn felt himself being pulled back from the window. Hannah said, 'Careful, he's one of the Cullens.'

They crept into the kitchen. Glenn prayed he wouldn't stab a toe in the dark and make some noise.

Still whispering, Hannah said, 'You need to go.'

Glenn said, 'You need to come with me.'

'I need to calm him down before he wakes the whole street.'

They heard the banging again, and the floorboards above them started shifting.

Glenn thought of what he could do. They could hide, as he had at the Jobcentre or in the street when he had met Hannah. Or he could call the police, of course, or get Hannah to do it, but he saw what happened in Spoons and it would defo happen again. He could run away, as he did on his bike, and leave her to her crazy Cullen ex, but he couldn't just leave her here.

Or he could stop running and hiding for once and do the right thing.

He said, 'You got a back garden, yeah?'

She showed him to the back door. He told her to lock it behind her, and he went to the back wall and climbed over into the alley. Then he walked down the longer end and around to the front of Hannah's street.

He could hear the knocking from eight houses away. He wasn't sure what was more of a concern, the thumping on the door or the thumping from his chest.

The Cullen had a fist on the door and he was leaning his head against it. Glenn felt like his heart was about to start mainlining. He stuck to the pavement and said, 'You OK there, buddy? Lost your key, is it?'

The Cullen stayed still. Glenn started to wonder if this was not actually that good an idea.

Glenn took slow steps closer, and then he said, 'Hey, don't I know you?'

The Cullen turned round.

Glenn felt sure that he was about to be ripped apart at the ribcage. But then he noticed the Cullen's arm. The one that was held across his chest. It was dripping blood.

Glenn said, 'Mate, please, let me have a look at your arm. That looks serious.'

He got closer. The cut ran the length of the Cullen's forearm. Glenn wondered if he'd been glassed after they left the Spoons.

The Cullen said, in a voice that almost sounded too small for him, 'I just wants to see my ex.'

Glenn looked at his arm. He understood what it was now. His cut was a cry for attention in physical form. Cullen wanted to show her and say, look, this is what I feel.

He didn't have long. Glenn took off his jumper and took off his T-shirt and put the jumper back on. Then he folded the tee and held it against Cullen's arm and said, 'You need to keep up the pressure.'

Cullen looked at him and said, 'I remembers you now. Sorry about the other day, I was havin a bad mornin. I just had a barney with my ex again, the one who lives here.'

And Glenn swallowed and said, 'No problem.'

It was starting to make sense. Cullen wasn't waiting for him as he chugged. He was waiting to speak to Hannah. Glenn thought of how Mim talked about this Cullen and wondered what Mim would think if he could see him now, broken and drunk and pining for someone who cared for him but didn't love him anymore.

Glenn was just about to suggest that the Cullen got his cut seen to when the Cullen looked up and said, 'You smell tha?'

Glenn said, 'No.'

The Cullen looked at Glenn and lowered his chin and said, 'You smells like her.'

Glenn breathed in. He had to think of something, anything, before the Cullen put two and two together.

He said, 'Mate, no offense now, but I think you got her on the brain. I been workin in KFC all night. All I smell of is fried chicken and sweat.'

The Cullen looked at the floor. Glenn prayed he didn't notice that he wasn't in work clothes. But the guy was a mess.

Glenn thought about all his interactions he'd seen this Cullen have. At the Jobcentre, not being believed in the

Spoons, being ignored by his ex in the street, and his own interaction with him on the bike. Every single time, he wasn't in the wrong, and people never took him at his word. All he needed was a bit of understanding.

'You really need to get some stitches in that,' Glenn said quickly. 'Please, go to the main road and flag down a taxi. I don't wanna get involved but if your ex means that much to you then you should see her at your best, not in the middle of the night all covered in blood. You owe it to yourself to be your best around her.'

The Cullen stared at him.

Glenn stared back. If he could keep it up for a second or two without his knees giving in he might not even get smacked.

Finally, the Cullen said, 'Fuck it. You knows what, you're OK, you are, bro.'

Glenn walked with him to the street, and told the Cullen to take care as he walked in the opposite direction. Then Glenn walked back down the alley behind Hannah's street and jumped over her garden wall and knocked gently on the glass till she let him in the kitchen.

He wouldn't stay long. He would just tell her that everything would be OK, and make sure that she didn't feel as lonely as the Cullen.

The Nice Guy

She checked her phone again. Lucia looked across the plaza, but all she could see were the other stallholders trying to attract the first customers: the Korean family next door frying the leftovers from their prep, just to get the wok fires going; Ali at the Persian stall putting out free tasters on cocktail sticks of his pomegranate chicken; and the Breton crepe guys shouting over the yard as if they were stadium touts selling tickets. Still no sign of Jade.

She got back to writing that night's menu on the blackboard. She was rubbing out the Genoa salami from the list of extras, as she hadn't found the time to make it to the deli, when she noticed Jade, finally, walking past the Devon crab shack. Her hair was tied back this time, and not down and ready to fall into the Cubanos as they made them. As Jade got closer, Lucia noticed she was carrying two small, cloudy glasses with rims of white and circles of lime wedged on.

'Sorry I'm late,' Jade said.

Lucia looked down at the glasses and said, 'What the hell are these?'

Jade smiled. 'Just some frozen margaritas.'

Lucia tried not to frown.'We have plenty of time to drink later.'

'They were free and they're tasty. The guys who work in the big top bar are really nice.'

Jade walked past and went into the back of the van. Lucia heard two clicks, and the canopy went up and she pulled it

74

into place. Jade put the straw to her lips. Lucia shook her head and went round the back to join her. 'You could have at least got espresso martinis,' she said, as Jade handed her a drink.

They fell into the groove. Reggaeton boomed out from the open-sided big top, and people were coming up to their van and having a look at the menu. A few had enquired about weddings and match days at rugby clubs, two things they hadn't done yet. Two young men, one with an undercut, and the other with tattoos down his arms and a backwards baseball cap, walked up to the van. The man with the undercut had a sternness to his face; Lucia couldn't tell if he was hangry and unaware of it or if he frowned as default. He looked over at the van and Lucia saw him look at Jade and smile.

'This is the one,' the man said, as he walked towards the van. 'I'm telling you, Harry, the Cubanos they make are the best thing ever. It's like a long posh ham and cheese toastie but with mustard and pickles. Jade brought me one over last Sunday and I've been dreaming about them all week.'

'That's great, Orlando, but we've only got ten minutes and you know I don't eat scorched animal flesh. Or coagulations made from the juice of a cow's udder,' the guy called Harry said.

They stared at the menu on the chalk board. 'We can make you one with facon and cashew cheese,' Lucia said. 'We even keep a plancha vegan-only so it's not cooked on the same griddle.'

'Sold,' the man called Orlando said, and Lucia put on a fresh pair of blue vinyl gloves.

Harry turned around – to look for seats, Lucia thought – but she noticed that Orlando stayed facing forward. His eyes were fixed on Jade's body when she leaned over to pass the food through the counter. Lucia reckoned that for all she knew he could have been watching her in silence for the whole two minutes in which they were prepping the Cubanos. He smiled, then said to Jade, 'We'll be over at the far corner near the bonfire.'

Orlando smiled at both of them and walked away. Lucia waited for Jade to unzip the front of her apron and put the money in but she was still watching the two men walk off to the benches near the overhanging heat lamps and burn barrels. She said, 'Did you even charge them?'

Jade crossed her arms and said, 'They gave us those frozen margaritas so it was a fair swap.'

Lucia wished that they could have a quiet spell to talk, but the plaza was full of curious people looking at their van and checking out the menu. 'Please don't do that again,' she said. 'The markup on cocktails is huge compared to ours. And what was that about the bonfire?'

Jade said, 'They get off at eleven tonight. They were asking if we wanna go for a drink.'

'And you said yes?'

'Of course, they're nice guys.'

Lucia took her gloves off, and turned to serve a woman in a stripy bobble hat and thick-rimmed glasses. She tried not to think about walking home late after a few drinks with all that night's takings.

They served a steady stream over the next hour and a half. Other stalls that had more workers, like the Korean family next door with their trademark napa kimchi tofu box, might go right on until midnight, but Lucia always felt it was best they got out before the collective blood alcohol content hit its critical level. They wouldn't even make as much in the last ninety minutes as they would in the first half-hour when the gates opened. At half past ten they brought down the canopy, latched it to the side, and turned off the planchas. They were out and apron-free by eleven on the dot.

They walked through the noisy crowd. A couple of customers recognised them and nodded as they walked past. Lucia couldn't see the guys Jade was looking for. She was just about to suggest that they go to the bar again when Lucia saw Orlando shoot up a hand. She wondered for a second if she could get away with not telling Jade, but she had already made eye contact with him. She nudged Jade, who was looking the other way, and they went over.

They had managed to get one of the benches closest to the bonfire. Orlando had a cigarette in his mouth. Lucia couldn't tell if his eyes were thin from the smoke in his face or if they were half-closed because of how drunk he was.

Jade got talking with Orlando straight away. Harry offered a hand out and formally introduced himself. She had to wipe the sweat from his palm on her jeans after they shook. Before they could speak properly, Jade turned to Lucia and said, 'Margarita again?'

Lucia nodded, and Jade got up. Orlando said, 'Your round, buddy,' and Harry sighed under his breath and stood.

Lucia watched them walk off. Then Orlando turned to her and said, 'So you're a half-caste, are you? I love that your skin and eyes are the same light brown. And your hair, you have so much hair. It's like you've got dreads. I bet you go black under the sun.'

She looked at him and realised that he wasn't joking. It was the most boring question she was ever asked – though normally it was asked in a more culturally sensitive way – and she had been asked variations of it so many thousands of times throughout her life that she had even developed a stock answer. The truth was that she had grandparents from all over the place, from Cape Verde to Istanbul to Coleraine. Such was the nature, she often found, of people who came from port cities. But it was late and she had been working all day, and she had no desire to entertain. 'I'm from the Docks,' she said, wishing it was her round.

'I think you're really pretty,' he said. 'Most half-castes are a bit, you know, but you seem to have a bit of class.'

Orlando turned to face her straight on. She had to move back slightly because his breath smelled like a farm. She wanted to leave, to get up and find Jade and say that this man was a prick, but she saw Jade and Harry behind Orlando, each carrying two drinks. They sat back down at the table. 'It's so busy in here,' Jade said.

'Just as well I can go behind the bar at the big top,' Harry said. 'Or we'd still be three deep.'

'Sorry, Lucia, but we owe them at least another Cubano each now,' Jade said, and she laughed.

'Lucia was just telling me about her exotic origins,' Orlando said. 'Her English is so good.'

Lucia looked at Jade. She had one of those faces like someone had just taken off a sock they'd been wearing all day and rubbed it in her face. Harry caught Lucia's eyes, and slowly shook his head.

Lucia said, 'If you wanna see how good my English is then you're going the right way about it.'

But Orlando leaned in closer to her and said, 'Kitchen or hotel? You people always work in one of them. Or you might even work in a hotel kitchen, yeah?'

He laughed to himself. From the other side of the table, Harry looked over at Orlando and said, 'Oh for fuck's sake, you're always doing this. Would you please just SHUT FUCKING UP.'

Lucia watched Orlando swing his head in a long arc until he was looking at Harry. He said, 'OK, mate. It was just a bit of banter.'

'I love how when Lucia told you to stop you ignored her,' Harry said. 'But when a man is doing it you actually listen.'

Orlando put out his cigarette on the table and said, 'Christ, mate. Stop being a dick.'

Harry turned to look at Lucia and said, 'Am I being a dick?'

Lucia said, 'You're definitely not the one being a dick.'

'Fuck all of you,' Orlando said, and he got up, pushing himself up off his knees. 'I hope someone scratches the shit out of your van.'

They watched him walk off, not quite in a straight line, almost tripping over a group sat down in a circle near the bonfire.

'So sorry you had to go through that,' Harry said. 'He's a lot nicer when he's sober. I know it's the most clichéd thing to say, but I hope you know not all men are like that.'

'Not All Men,' Lucia said while looking at Jade, and they laughed.

Harry was smiling. 'What I'm trying to say,' he said, 'is that it took me a long, long time to check my privilege and learn to be an actual nice guy and not just trash.'

'It's fine. I wish more guys were like you. Right, Jade?'

Jade took a sip of her margarita. Harry said, 'I had best go off and find him. Would you mind holding my seat? I won't bring him back.'

Lucia nodded. They watched him walk off. 'I can't believe that creep,' Jade said.

'I know. I hope he doesn't come back.'

Lucia thought Orlando was so drunk that if she texted Albanian Benny on the gate his description he would get knocked round like an Eton mess and chucked on the street. She was going to suggest it but Jade said, 'He kept on trying to kiss my hand. So slimy.'

Lucia tried not to grimace. She thought Jade had offered to get the round of margaritas in when they sat down cos Jade was a borderline alkie, not because Orlando had tried to hold

79

her hand. But before she replied, Harry came back and sat down. 'He wasn't at the bar or in the portaloos. I popped my head in the plaza but forgot to check your van,' he said.

Lucia got up. 'I have to see,' she said, and she stepped over the seat.

'I'll come with,' Jade said, and she stood.

'Save the bench. I'm probably just being paranoid.'

'Yeah, Jade, keep me company,' Harry said, and he pulled her by the hand and Jade sat back down.

He said something in her ear. So that's the way this is going, Lucia thought, as she walked off. 'I'll see you in a sec,' she called back, but she could see that Jade was too busy trying to hear what Harry was saying over the crowd to notice.

She got to the plaza, empty except for the wife and husband team putting their pad thai woks away in the back of their tuk-tuk. She got her phone out and checked the outside of the van. No scratches, no scrapes, still striped blue and white. She went round the front and the lone star still had five points and it sat smooth on the bonnet in its bold red triangle. Then, knowing that she would eventually come back if she went without checking inside, she walked round the side and climbed the two steps to the van door and unlocked it. She turned on the light, and saw that the two plancha griddles, microwave and prep counters were all as they'd left them, as were the takings under the counter they'd bagged up ready for the bank tomorrow. She was about to head out when she heard a knock at the back door, and she thought, finally, Jade has had enough too.

She opened the door, and was about to suggest that they catch a taxi back to hers to drop off the takings before going to see if Mischiefs was still open down the Docks, but Harry was in front of her, hands in pockets and looking cold.

'Sorry to disturb you,' he said. 'I was hoping I caught you here.'

He took the two steps up and stayed in the doorway of the van. Lucia took a step back so he wasn't in her personal space.

'Is Jade OK? Did Orlando come back?'

'She's fine. She went over to the big top bar. I said I would come get you. It's just you and me here now.'

She could feel his eyes on her. She wanted to peel her skin off. She said, 'I'm going to find Jade, make sure she's OK.'

'We should stay here. Just me and you. I could tell by the way you looked at me when Orlando called you exotic that we want the same thing.'

She thought, sure, we want the same thing if that thing is you leaving me the fuck alone. But instead she said, 'I don't think we do.'

He stepped forward and grabbed her hand. It was as sweaty as it was before. She tried pulling it away but he held tighter. Then he bent over and brought her hand up and kissed it.

She felt her skin go cold, and she pulled her hand away, sliding through his in the sweat. She thought back to what Jade had said. *He tried to kiss my hand. So slimy.* Jade wasn't talking about Orlando back at the benches.

She wished he would stop staring at her. 'You said not all men are bad, but now you're acting like this,' she said.

'Give me a chance,' he said. 'I'm a nice guy. I'm so nice I should be called Harry Krishna.'

He was looking down at her body. She hated it when men did that. She thought Harry must know how rapey it was to check her out right after they'd locked eyes, but then she remembered he was a Nice Guy.

'I'm not looking for anyone right now,' she said, after a second or two. 'I've got too much going on with the van.'

She hoped he would get the hint but he didn't move. She always felt like she had some kind of responsibility to not make the guy feel bad about turning him down. But in the space they were in with the shutter down, she knew it was because she didn't know what could happen.

He said, 'But you have absolutely no reason to turn me down. You're young, I'm young, and we're both single. We have things in common like the fact that we both work in the same place.'

She wanted to say that no, you work *for* someone, while I work for myself. She wished she had listened when Jade suggested they do the festival circuit, driving from Boomtown to Primavera to Outlook, selling Cubanos along the way. She could be on the Punta Christo road by now and not cornered and scared where nobody knew where she was.

'It's still a no,' she said. 'Let's go and find Jade.'

He sighed and said, 'Look, at the end of the day, you're lucky I chose you and not Jade.'

'OK, now we definitely need to go.'

She tried to push past him but he stayed still. She felt a wave of terror rise up from her stomach and she thought, no, not this, and he tried to grab her waist. She pushed him off, but he grabbed her hand and he stepped closer. Then she looked behind him and noticed Jade at the door. She thought Jade herself must think something is going on so she shook her head and Jade made a push motion with both her hands. She pulled her wrist out of Harry's hand before he could even think to hold it tighter, and she slammed the heel of both palms into his shoulders. The force of the shove made him step back, and she thought he was going to hold his balance, but then he fell back through the door. He almost seemed to go up for a second, and Lucia saw that Jade was bending down and he had fallen over her.

She heard a smack as he hit the floor. She rushed to the door and looked outside. He was lying on his front. His legs and arms were spread and bent like he was trying to make himself into a swastika.

'Is he breathing?' Lucia said. She stepped down from the van.

They stood there, watching him. Lucia squatted and looked at his face in the gravel. She could see red and bits of stone stuck to the underside of his face. Jade said, 'I don't care.'

Lucia put her head closer and heard a small groan. She stood back up before she disturbed him. 'I thought you were at the big top bar.'

'I thought dudebro here was going to the toilet but when he didn't come back I thought I had best come and find you. I told you he was slimy.'

They watched him on the floor. Slowly, after a moment, he started to shift and he rolled over onto his back. He moaned again and sat up, and brushed the gravel off his face. He looked at the grey and red that was stuck to his palm.

'Let's go,' Jade said.

Lucia went to the van. She locked the door. She felt like picking up the step and making sure that he hit the floor again. She wasn't going anywhere this time. She was getting tired. She didn't even care anymore: she was just tired of it happening. She was tired of being thought of as a piece of meat in a butcher's window, tired of being thought of as two disparate halves of two racial wholes. The nice guys and the bigots could all fuck the fuck off.

Jade motioned to leave, but Lucia ignored her. She stayed staring down at Harry as he rubbed something out of his eye. Then he said, 'I've never been pushed over by a girl before.'

'If you want to get pushed over again then stand back up,' Lucia said.

Jade put her hand on Lucia's arm but she brushed her off.

'I can't believe you friend-zoned me,' he said, as he made to get back up. 'I always get friend-zoned.'

Lucia pushed him down on the shoulders so he couldn't move. She went to speak, but Jade got there first.

'She's not your friend,' Jade said. 'She's mine. And I'll tell you this now, if she was to ever somehow become your friend it wouldn't be some kind of runner-up prize, you fucking creep.'

'You're both the same as the rest of them. I don't understand why women are attracted to arseholes when they could have a nice guy.'

'Yeah, of course, it's my fault. You're playing the victim here.'

He looked up at Lucia, and then at Jade. Lucia crossed her arms.

'It's OK. I understand. I'm a bit of a feminist.'

He got up and walked away. When he rounded the van, Jade and Lucia looked at each other. Lucia shook her head. 'Nice Guys never learn,' she said.

They went and found a bench and got some more margaritas, hoping they didn't bump into any more Nice Guys for at least the rest of the night.

The Visit

Right after the ID check and the dog sniff and the pat-down, the big screw with the chest like a slab of sirloin goes through the rules again. No touching. No hugging. No kissing.

We leaves the waiting room and walks through to the visiting hall. Each con waits at a separate table. They're all wearing orange bibs to show that they were the ones who got caught. Everyone finds the brother or the boyfriend or the spar they were looking for and no one gives a fuck about what the big screw just said.

Collins always likes to play it cool. When he offers his fist for a spud I bats him away and makes him stand up. I hugs him like I'm trying to get lost in his cleavage.

When we lets go, the couple on the table next to us are still going at it. He's got a plain grey tee on under his orange bib, and she's wearing a black strapless top and two gold eyebrow hoops. She hovers slightly above him as they tear into each other's gums. They're necking so hard that she looks like a gannet trying to retch some fish guts into his mouth.

We sits down. I clocks Collins for the first time in three months. You can really notice the size he's put on. He'd chafe his shoulders trying to get through most doors now. And even his wrists look as thick as my thighs.

'Fair play. You're lookin hench,' I says. 'You're gettin on for bein the biggest Welsh guy I knows. If you pumps up any more, we'll have to start callin you Aled Schwarzenegger.'

Collins looks pleased, and lets out a bit of a smile.

'It's all the bread,' he says. 'We gets three meals a day, but they always fills up a serving table with loaves and loaves of bread. I just makes sure I has a loaf with every meal. You knows what it's like, bro. There ain't nothin else to do here apart from watch telly or work out.'

'You could try writing more letters.'

He feels the back of his head, where his hair is shortest. 'People lies with words. They makes up all sorts of stories. If you got something you wants to say, you has to say it to my face. Chantelle comes round once a week anyway, and sometimes I gets a visit from my Mumma and all.'

And as he leans back, all you can think is it might be easy enough to lie when you're hiding behind some words, but it's easier to get away with it when you're face to face and you can hide behind a mask.

'So what you got to say en bro,' he carries on. 'I best not have wasted a visitin slot if you're just gonna whine on about how I ain't written you a letter.'

He smiles, and you thinks to yourself that in twenty minutes' time he's gonna wish that's all we been talking about.

'Right then. I'll start right at the beginning,' I says. 'It all kicked off about this time last week.'

* * *

You goes proper deep into your swede to tell the story. You sets the scene, exactly as it happened, and gives him a running real-time commentary.

You tells your spar how you'd not long woken up that afternoon. Mumma is downstairs and you're just weighing up some contraband in case you has to go on a mission. There's a knock at the door so you goes down and answers

86

it. Straight away you wishes you hadn't cos there waiting on the street is Evo Lynch. And seeing that scum with the teardop under his eye and the scars around his neck don't half make you have to brace your knees. But even if you had ignored the knock, Mumma's always got the telly on extra loud when she tidies up so he probably woulda heard the screaming domestic on the chat show she's half-watching anyway.

So you carries on and tells Collins that he got the right idea, renting a different place every coupla months after each crop finishes and fucking off before the bills come in, cos then no twonkey knows where you lives. Stick in the same house all your life and word gets round, standard.

So you tells him how it went down.

'Sapnin brer,' Evo says. 'Long time, long time.'

You looks at him but the last thing you wants is him casing out your joint to find stuff to come back for later. You keeps your face straight and says, 'Safe, bro. Standard.'

And he wastes no time at all. 'Brer, I needs a favour, I does. I'm late and I got to get up Pentrebane on the double.'

'Gone Ely in five, bro. Go see my new girlfriend.'

Which is almost true, cos Lisa had been texting you earlier, and wanted you to come and chill. And you were half thinking about it cos you got a few hours to waste. It was a Tuesday and Kyle wouldn't be there. And she must still be keen cos she's still sending you messages even though you ain't seen her in a few weeks cos you started seeing someone else.

You hopes with that he'll get the message and fuck off, but he looks over your shoulder and opens a nostril to get a better sniff. You hopes his beak has picked up the cut grass out the back garden, cos behind you at the end of the kitchen the door is wide open. If he's smelling the other grass you been weighing and cutting up in your bedroom, you and the old dear are in trouble.

But instead he says, 'Standard, brer. If you're gone Ely anyway, you can drop me off at my boy's school. It ain't far. Top end of Pentrebane. Right by the top shops. Practically on your way.'

'Let's go en, bro,' you say, before he got the chance to sniff. 'Best be off now if we wants to make it before your kid leaves school.'

You steps out the house without even telling Mumma wha gwaan. You hopes later on when you goes to see your new girl that she don't realise you're wearing six-month-old trainers.

We gets in the car, and takes a left onto Lansdowne Road. We bombs it down to the Ely roundabout, flying past all the pubs and MOT garages on the way. After bombing into Fairwater, Evo's swede slowly turns to look at you. His eyes are burning through your temple, and you misses second gear twice and almost stalls the engine.

You wants to say to him that we're in suburban land, and he should be clocking all the nice bungalows and semis cos it's the type of place where they leaves their kitchen doors open all night. But instead you say, 'Chill, bro. We'll be there in five, standard. We're almost at the Pentrebane hill now. Have a smoke in the glove compartment. No need to worry.'

But he just keeps staring at you, and every time your pulse pumps it feels like he's scooping out a little bit more from your noggin.

'I needs a spliff I does,' he says. 'I gets nervous when I sees my son, brer. My boy don't know yet how bad of a father I really am.'

You thinks about the two turbo spliffs you made for when you goes to see your new girl later, and wonders if that's the type of thing that Evo needs right now. But his looking starts to get you nervous so you says, 'Standard, bro. There's some in the fag pack in the glove compartment.'

So he sparks up the magic wand and has a few puffs. He smells the smoke coming off the cherry, which fills the car up with the bitterness that crack, weed and tobacco brings. You knows he recognises the smell cos he practically takes the rest down in one lungful.

His head starts going up and down like he's agreeing with something. 'I knows what you're thinkin,' he says. 'You thinks I'm a bad father for smokin then going to pick up my boy.'

You makes an effort to steady the tone of your voice, and not to be too enthusiastic in your answer.

'No, bro. I bet you're a good father, standard.'

'I learnt bad habits, see. Me and my ex didn't mean to have my son. Then I basically did what my old man did to me. When I was a nipper, he looked my Mumma bang in the face and said he'd be back at closin time. She never saw him again. And I ain't much better either.'

We drives without chatting for the half-mile climb up Gorse Place, and turns past the flats onto Beechley Drive, the last part of the hill and the first point of Pentrebane.

As you parks outside the chippy at the top shops, you goes to take off your seatbelt but Evo stops you. He puts his hood on and pulls all the strings, so all that is showing on his face is the mole to the right of his beak. He pulls your hood over your own noggin, then flumps it into the steering wheel. We stays like that for a second or two, then he lets go. Before you gets the chance to ask him very politely What The Fuck, you looks past all the Mummas going to wait for their nippers and you sees someone familiar about thirty feet away. It's Chantelle, and even though her hair is scraped back and she ain't done her face yet, she's still looking beautiful. She's wearing a tight pair of grey jeggings and some tan sheepskin boots. It looks like she's dressing to impress someone later on.

She looks round but don't clock us, and walks into the chippy. 'I really can't be arsed,' Evo says. 'That girl ain't nothin but trouble.'

You ain't sure if it's the sight of Chantelle or the magic ingredient in the wand he just had, but Evo's sweating so hard he looks like he's basted himself up for a jailbreak.

'I dunno why you doesn't wanna say hi,' you says. 'She's safe, she is. Mint and all.'

His smile is all cracked and yellow. He says, 'Someone got a crush.'

You tries to think about how to put this in a way he'll understand, and in the end you says, 'Come on, bro. She's special, that one. Everyone fancies her. She's one in a mill, standard.'

He looks out the window and says it himself. 'One in a mill.'

And he just stares, and you thinks that maybe you ain't dropped the tone low enough for Evo to understand. So you tries again by saying, 'You knows what I means, bro. She's one of those girls who's so fit you'd actually pay good money to suck the last dick that fucked her.'

He takes his hood down. The way his face is set makes him look like the front end of a Chinese Dragon.

'If you knows what I does, brer of mine, you wouldn't be sayin that to me.'

'Well no, spar,' you says back, even though you're only now coming round to the idea that Evo is more woke than you've ever given him credit for. 'I dunno what's going on in your swede.'

* * *

You're back in the visiting room again with Collins. The couple to our left are still going at it, forcing their tongues down each other's throats. You wonders if they carries on like this whether you'll catch a bit of tit out the corner of your eye. You has to stop a minute to take a big gulp of air, cos you got to the bit where you can't look at Collins in the face while you tells the rest of the story.

You breathes in and out and takes your spar back to that afternoon last week.

* * *

You're in the car with Evo, and Chantelle is putting a bag of chips on the passenger seat of her car across the road. You looks away when she bends down cos you were staring. 'Put it this way,' Evo says. He breathes out smoke and you can feel the spots forming on your forehead already. 'We got a special type of relationship, me and Chantelle. She might be trouble, but I got feelins for my girl there, and my girl there got feelins for me. So the more you talks about her like that, the more I feels like I wants to pick your nose with my big toe.'

With that, Evo gets out the car and walks down the street to pick his nipper out of school.

You stops the story again and looks at Collins. He's gone all shoulders and no neck. You've added fifteen years to his face already.

The guy to your left has his hands around the back of his Mrs's swede. She's leaning over the table, her gut just about sitting down on the surface. You realises that they haven't talked all session. Just tongued like they might not ever see each other again.

You tells your spar the rest quick-time, before he got a chance to think. Evo comes out, and his kid is running in front of him in his red and white school uniform. He's all streaked with mud and grass stains. You tells your spar how you ain't sure what was bigger, the little nipper or the bag on his back.

When the kid gets closer, you realises that you recognises the crew cut and the gaps where the milk teeth have fallen out. Then you realises that you are in a bad situation, like when you're halfway through a piss and the toilet seat lid falls down.

Before you gets a chance to put your own hood up, the nipper is looking through the passenger seat window. 'Oh look,' he says. 'It's the big scaredy-cat.'

Evo clips him on the crown. The nipper looks up at his old man. 'SHURRUP Kyle,' Evo says. 'I thought your Mumma taught you manners.'

And the kid goes quiet and says, 'But that's what Mumma calls him. She told me he was a big scaredy-cat and he ran away.'

Nothing more is said until Kyle is buckled up in the back with the belt strap cut across his neck and Evo is all in your face like a wasp. 'So then, Kyle,' he says as he turns to face his son. 'I guess I doesn't have to tell you my man's name then, if you knows it already.'

And the kid drops you like you was two stone on a crash diet. 'This is Mumma's special friend,' he says. 'He comes round and he brings pizzas and they even lets me have my own one, but I doesn't like it when he comes round cos I has to go to bed early.'

Evo looks over. His face barely moves as he talks.

'It's only been three months,' he says.

'It ain't like that,' you says. 'I didn't know Lisa was your kid's Mumma. She never told me, she didn't want me to

92

know. And nothing's happening, it's all over. I got a new girl now, I swears down.'

You starts the engine, reverses, and before Evo got a chance to function you're through Pentrebane and heading back down Fairwater. You knows that if the nipper weren't in the back singing the Peppa Pig theme tune to himself then Evo would have stomped you so hard his knee would be in your throat.

As you gets to the shops down Fairwater Green, you realises that Evo's been looking at you the whole time.

'Pull over. I needs a can to cool off,' he says.

You stops the car on the side of the road and Evo offers out a palm. You slaps it with a tenner before he has to ask. He gets out and goes into the shop. You thinks how it ain't that far on a bus to Riverside, So you looks back at the nipper on the back seat and says, 'Kyle, go ask your Dada for some sweets. Go on, son.'

He wriggles out underneath the seat belt and lets himself out. As soon as he's in the shop, your engine is back on, and you're headed back towards the Ely roundabout. You doesn't look in the rear view mirror until you gone round two bends.

* * *

You stops your story there. When you gets your head back into the prison hall, you realises that your spar ain't really been listening for the last few minutes. There's no way of telling if he's cool about it or if he's swimming up an Egyptian river.

'I ain't made none of that up,' I says. 'Sorry you has to find out like this, bro.'

You looks at your hands and you looks at his face, and you can't tell who's more nervous.

'But she was here last week,' he says. 'There was none of this. Everything was normal.'

And all you can think is that the only reason why things were normal is cos Chantelle bottled it.

But before you has to say anything else, the guy and his Mrs to your left starts shouting. The big screw from the waiting room has his arms around her, and he's pulling her out of her seat. The guy stands up, but another meaty screw blows a whistle, and the guy sits down. On a tannoy, everyone is told to stay sat and still. The guy puts his hands on the table, then pulls his fingers in, scratching the table as he goes. You sees him swallow and almost choke, and you knows that he is probably gonna spend the next forty-eight hours in solitary with nothing for company except a bucket.

'Amateurs,' I whispers to Collins. 'She should be on the other side of the wall with a sixty quid drone from Argos.'

But Collins ain't really clocking what's going on.

No one in the room says a word. When the big screw comes back after taking the woman away, he's carrying a pair of handcuffs. 'Don't worry,' he says to the guy in the Liverpool shirt. 'We're gonna rip that right back out of you.'

Back outside in the real world, the sun is out but there ain't no heat. I walks through the car park and gets in my car. The driver's side is already open. I gets in and turns to look at my new girl. Her hair is scraped back but she got her face on, cos she knew she was seeing me today. She gives me a peck on the cheek.

'Did you tell him?' Chantelle says.

'Yes.'

'Did you tell him everything?'

'Yes.'

Collins heard nothing but the truth. But what he might not have heard is how after you fucked off from Evo and his nipper you went straight round Chantelle's house and started to curse her out and asked her how many guys she got on the go at the same time. And then how she said stop being a dick, I got feelins for him and he got feelins for me cos he's my fuckin cousin and I ain't no cousin fucker. Now you best go and pick him and Kyle back up before he bricks your living room window.

Chantelle smiles as I puts the car into gear and drives off. Just like Collins, she don't have to hear it all. He don't like sending letters and she won't be hearing from him anyhow. And as I smiles back at her, all I can think of is how lucky I am that I got my mask on.

Yes Kung Fu

Here's the thing. I'm flying past all the charity shops and kebab houses on Cowbridge Road when the grey Corsa in front of me stops straight up. Half a second later and my Clio is three inches from the boot and I'm all jacked up with war hormones. The Audi behind me does the same, and in my mirror I can see the big bald driver cursing me out something raw.

Get out the fuckin way, I goes to the Corsa. I'm late already. I can't be late today. But the Corsa don't move. It starts rocking. I honks my horn like it's gonna make a difference, but the Corsa just stays there.

I opens my door to go ask the goober in front of me what the fuck. The big bald guy behind me honks his horn again. You can see the traffic building up where Cowbridge Road snakes back towards town. All the shoppers on the pavement are watching. But my car is way too close. I couldn't turn round even if I wanted to. All I can really do is find out why the Corsa driver had to stop like that and tell them to fucking move.

And that's when I sees him.

Kung Fu is in front of the Corsa. He's wearing a white string vest and blue denim cut-offs. He's karate-chopping the Corsa's silver bonnet, right in the middle of the street. Slam after slam after slam.

I marches over towards the driver's side. The window is down. It's some young woman with two nippers in the back.

She got her hair scraped into a bun. She can't be older than twenty-three, and the nippers are bawling almost as loud as their Mumma is yelling.

Don't worry, I goes to her. It's only Kung Fu. I known him time. I'll talk to him now.

Everyone knows Kung Fu. There ain't no point asking him what his real name is. His name is Kung Fu now.

I turns to face him. Just about everyone got their own Kung Fu genesis story. Some say cops were raiding his flat once and he had to munch a sheet of acid before they found it. Others say he answered the door and his vindictive ex-missus slammed him eight times across the swede with a pot plant. Go up to anyone walking past you in town and ask them why Kung Fu got to sing at the cemetery gates all night or why he does the backstroke down to the Black Weir every Sunday and they'll all give you a different answer.

Yes, bro, he goes.

Yes, Kung Fu, I answers back.

That God up there. He is speaking to me, electronically. He don't like the grey.

He points at the car.

No, Kung Fu, I goes. It ain't God talking to you. It's me, your spar Tommo. We used to chill down the park when I was sellin a draw, remember. God don't mind about the colour of the car, I swears down.

Kung Fu is one of those people who everyone knows. There's at least one Kung Fu in every town. A few in each quarter of every city. Some people don't even believe that people like Kung Fu actually exist. They should be careful. The Kung Fu where they live is probably them.

The woman gets out of the car and starts shouting at Kung Fu to get out the way. A few cars down, this green bus lets off its horn. You can't tell which is loudest.

Don't worry, I goes to her. I knows what it's like. I got a little one too. I'm on my way to see her now.

That's the thing with Kung Fu. He might look all Zulu with his knuckled brown torso and his long clinching stare, but he don't mean no harm. Even when he ain't been taking his meds. Some people just is how they is.

She looks at me for a second like she don't give a fuck about what I been saying. Then she sits back in her car. When she gets her phone out you know that in ten seconds' time she'll be on the line to the law.

I only got one thought. They can't come now. I needs to see them later. If it's a copper I knows then they might even be aware of the warrant, and then I won't get to see Tasha one last time. I'll be straight on remand this time and there ain't no way Angela will ever let her see me doing bird.

I goes into the inside pocket of my jacket. I gets out half of one of the bundles I was saving to give to Angela for when I gets put away.

Look, that's more than enough for the bumps in your bonnet, I goes. He's my problem now. I'm gonna take him away, and you can carry on drivin. It's all gonna be safe.

I reaches through the window and presses the wad into her hand. Her fingers can barely close around it. She looks at me as if I was more mad than Kung Fu. Then she does the window up and slowly edges forward.

Kung Fu, get in my fuckin car, I goes.

I starts my engine. She still hasn't quite driven away enough. The cars behind me starts beeping again. I catches up just as she indicates and pulls over outside a bakery. You know she's gonna call the law anyway. I presses my foot down and goes into fourth. We just about makes it through the traffic lights at Vicky Park.

Fuckin hell, Kung Fu, I goes. You don't half pick your fuckin moments.

You are not my support worker, he goes.

No, Kung Fu. I ain't your support worker.

Jo Hopkins is my support worker.

Yes, Kung Fu. Jo Hopkins is your support worker.

This car, it just too small. Where is my Jo Hopkins.

I don't know, Kung Fu. You tell me.

Kung Fu gives me the name of a hostel. It's one of those Care in the Community places where he must live. It's just around the corner from the flat where my ex lives with Tasha.

I turns to face him as we gets to the Ely roundabout.

Five minutes, Kung Fu. Five minutes and we'll be there. I'll drop you off and you can go see Jo Hopkins.

We turns through into Fairwater and starts climbing the hill to Pentrebane. Kung Fu goes through my glove compartment where I keeps all my pocket stuff. He sparks up a smoke and starts inspecting my phone like it was full of clues to something. His questions are non-stop. I can't believe the sentences that are coming out of my mouth.

No, Kung Fu. I can't drop you off in Arundel.

No, Kung Fu. That's a cigarette, not a weapon of mass destruction.

No, Kung Fu. If you dial 666 the phone won't be answered by Mephistopheles.

He gets more and more agitated by the small space. And the negative answers ain't really doing it for him either.

Just as we gets to Beechley Drive and the last drag up to the flats, Kung Fu undoes his seatbelt.

Let me out, he goes. I need to find Jo Hopkins.

You might as well stay in, I goes. Save your legs for the last part up this hill.

I gets to the junction and comes to a stop to let this slow car go first. Just as I'm about to drive off, Kung Fu opens his door and steps out.

Fuckin hell, Kung Fu, I goes. You coulda given me some warnin. I almost took off with half you still sat down.

But Kung Fu don't notice. He just starts walking back down the hill, away from where his hostel is. I thinks about going and grabbing him, but then I realises that time is running out if I wants to see Tasha. And Kung Fu ain't my problem now. I done my good bit on Cowbridge Road.

I pulls into the residents' car park and leaves a note on the window. I goes into my glove compartment to get my smokes and phone, but they ain't there. Damn, I'm thinking. It's that Kung Fu. He musta taken them. He can be such a fucking tea leaf. But it ain't really his fault. He's one of those people who got no understanding of possession. That's why he's always wearing such mad clothes, cos he just puts other people's on all the time and walks away.

As I gets out the car, I makes a mental note to go find out who Jo Hopkins is at the hostel. I can go find her after I seen Tasha. But Tasha is more important right now than my phone and smokes.

I gets to the block where they lives, and the front of the buzzer system is all smashed up. I hates it when this happens. It's always kids with nothing else to do or some dickhead with a stupid vendetta against someone in this block, spoiling life for the rest of us. I looks around and there ain't no one else about. I knocks on the nearest window but they doesn't answer. They must be used to this. The people on the ground floor never buzzes anyone in.

Tasha and Angela lives five floors up. I tries calling out but no one replies. Not even anyone to tell me to shut up.

Fuck, I am thinking. I got to find Kung Fu. If I doesn't find Kung Fu then I doesn't get to see Tasha. I must find him and get my phone. So Tasha or Angela can buzz me in.

I drives out of the estate and heads back down the hill. I

has to get my phone. Ever since Jamo down the line got busted, we all knew it was game over. And when you hears on the grapevine you got a warrant out on you, sometimes you just wants to say goodbye to the ones you love. Especially when you got a daughter as beautiful and sweet as Tasha. I can't let Kung Fu fuck it all up.

I'm halfway back down the hill, and then I sees him again. Kung Fu is at the side of the road. He's karate-chopping this lamppost. He takes a few steps back and does a flying kick. You can hear the hollow banging coming from the lamppost's metal front before you steps out of the car.

For fuck's sake, Kung Fu, I goes. It's only a fuckin lamppost. Leave it the fuck alone before someone calls the fuckin cops.

He turns to look at me.

Look, that God up there. He is speaking to me, electronically. He don't like the grey.

I grabs my face in my hand. It's all I can do to calm down.

Whatever, Kung Fu, I goes. Just give me my phone and my smokes. I got to see my daughter.

He puts his arms by his sides. I know what's going through his mind. Tasha don't mean fuck all to him. There's something grey here and God told him to get rid of it. That's all that matters.

Before I can think of anything else to say, I gets the feeling that I shoulda been paying more attention in other places. There's a siren going off, and it's getting closer. Someone must have heard Kung Fu having an epi with the lamppost and called the cops.

The police car pulls up across the other side of the road. My vital organs drop somewhere into my pelvis. I still ain't seen Tasha. If they recognises me, then I might not see her. And I was gonna hand myself in. I wasn't gonna run away to

Cyprus like the other boys. Maybe my ex will bring Tasha for a visit if I gets a local enough prison.

I'm thinking it's all over when Kung Fu grabs my shoulder. He's got that long clinching stare going on and I has to concentrate on the deep blue of his eyes.

Your name is Jo Hopkins, he goes. Your name is Jo Hopkins and you are my support worker. You're takin me back to the Hostel.

I don't even get a chance to ask what he's on about. The coppers gets out of their car but they leave the lights on. The younger one is about my age. He keeps his right hand back and on the truncheon attached to his waist. He thinks you doesn't notice this. The older one stays by the car and crosses his arms.

You can tell that they knows who Kung Fu is cos they speaks to me first. Alright there, mate, the younger one says. Everything OK, I hope.

They always starts like this. That's the thing with the law. You'll never meet anyone as polite as a copper who don't want you to know that he's two minutes away from arresting you.

I can feel my heart trying to escape from my ribcage. I ain't ever seen these two before. But if they works out who I am then they'll have me on lockdown before the end of my next breath.

Kung Fu nudges my shoulder. Something comes back to me. He already gave me the answer. My name is Jo Hopkins. Jo can be a bloke's name too.

It's all good, Officer, I goes. My name is Jo Hopkins and I work for Taff Housing Association. We were just on our way back to the hostel. He wandered out through the back door when I was on my tea break. No problems at all.

The copper stares at me like I just offered to shampoo his hair. I wonders if Jo Hopkins even works for the housing

102

association, or if I shoulda said that I works for the NHS or something instead.

Let's see some ID, the copper goes.

I pats myself down so I got time to think.

I just run straight out of the hostel, Officer. I must have left it on the desk.

They radios through to find out if a Jo Hopkins actually exists. I ain't got much time.

Come on, Officer, I tries again. You knows Kung Fu. Everyone knows what he's like. Let me take him back to the hostel. There ain't no damage done. People just gets paranoid. We doesn't need all this bother. You can come and check on him later if you like. I'll give you the address.

He looks at the older copper. There ain't no way of knowing how they communicates but after a few seconds he's shooing us away with one hand.

We gets in my car, does the world's worst eight-point turn as the coppers cross their arms and watch, and splutters back towards Pentrebane. I can feel how I needs to wipe the sweat off my forehead.

I ask Kung Fu for my phone and smokes. He puts them in the glove compartment.

You ain't really Jo Hopkins, he goes.

Yes, Kung Fu. I knows that. I'm your spar Tommo, remember. We'll go find Jo Hopkins now.

As he gets out the car outside his building, I works it all out. We ain't so different, me and Kung Fu. He needs Jo Hopkins like I needs Tasha.

Kung Fu walks away. He don't even wave. He passes a lamp post and it's as grey as an elephant, but he don't even attack it, cos he's gonna see Jo Hopkins in a second. I starts the engine as he knocks on a window, and I goes to say goodbye.

Notes

Earlier versions of some of these stories also appeared in the following places:

'The Pavement Poet' in *New Welsh Reader 117*, Summer 2018

'The Tea Party' in *Cheval 6: The Terry Hetherington Young Writer's Award Anthology 2012* (Parthian, 2012)

'The Anatomy of a Beating' in *New Welsh Review 100*, Summer 2013

'Asking a Shadow to Dance' in *Cheval 7: The Terry Hetherington Young Writer's Award Anthology 2013* (Parthian, 2013)

'Things That Make the Heart Beat Faster' first appeared as 'The Rave' in *Memorable Firsts* (Parthian, 2011)

'The Visit' in *A Fiction Map of Wales* (H'mm Foundation/Rhys Davies Trust, 2014)

'Yes Kung Fu' in *New Welsh Short Stories* (Seren, 2015)

Acknowledgements

These stories passed through lots of hands before they made their way into this collection. I owe a debt of gratitude to each person here for contributing their thoughts:

John Abell // Aida Birch // Emma Birch // Zillah Bowes // Rosey Brown // Gwen Davies // Richard Lewis Davies // Rhian Elizabeth // Matthew Francis // Robin Ganderton // Eluned Gramich // Katie Gramich // Niall Griffiths // Richard Gwyn // Phil Jones // John Lavin // Lucy Llewellyn // Catrin Kean // Rebecca Parfitt // Alan Perry // Jean Perry // Jem Poster // clare e. potter // Francesca Rhydderch // Richard Owain Roberts // Danny Rowland aka The Pavement Poet // Durre Shahwar // Abhishek Skihwal // Adam Christopher Smith // Penny Thomas // Louise Walsh // Rhys Owain Williams // Steve Yellen

Thank you all.

A special thanks to my editor, Susie Wild, for her committed and steadfast advice // care // time, which was of inimitable value in the creation of this book. It wouldn't have been the same collection without her.

Maciej Dakowicz is a Polish photographer and educator based in Poland and Thailand. He is a member of the international street photography collective In-Public and an official Fujifilm X-Photographer. His interests are in documentary, travel and street photography. Maciej's photos have been widely published, exhibited and shown at photo festivals. He is a recipient of numerous awards and has judged several photography competitions. Currently he is mainly occupied with teaching his street photography workshops in Asia and eastern Europe.